D0407166

A POWER BOYS ADVENTURE

The Mystery of

THE BURNING OCEAN

By Mel Lyle

Illustrated by
Raymond Burns

WHITMAN PUBLISHING COMPANY • Racine, Wisconsin

Racine, Wisconsin
Printed in the U.S.A. by
Western Printing and Lithographing Company

Contents

1 *Double Trouble*

"Let's get out of here, Jack," Chip Power said, already on his way out of the guesthouse.

"Okay," his older brother answered.

They passed the registration desk. Blaze, their Dalmatian, tagged along. The honeymoon couple, the boys saw, was still monopolizing the Ping-Pong table. On the screened porch, other guests played cards.

"Could you stand this place another day?" Chip asked as they stepped outside.

"Look at that sunset, would you?" Jack said, pointing at the swirling orange-and-charcoal sky. "You're not going to see anything like that in New York."

"You know what I want to do tomorrow—when we get to New York?"

"What?" Jack asked. They had started across the lawn. "Start wishing you were back in Bermuda?"

Blaze's growl stopped both boys. It came as a challenge from deep in the dog's throat. Blaze moved slowly, tensely forward. His tail was straight and stiff, on a line with his back.

"No, Blaze!" Chip ordered, grabbing the dog's collar. "No! Easy, boy!"

In the dusk of early evening the boys saw a man staggering along a shortcut from the bay to the guesthouse. He wore only a pair of swim trunks. His body was a dead white against the gray light.

"Wonder what's wrong with him?" Chip asked.

"Hold on to Blaze," Jack ordered. "I'm going to—"

"Looks like he's going to fall," Chip interrupted.

The man did fall and then lay motionless on his back.

Jack was already running. "Hold on to the hound!" he called back.

But Blaze tore free of Chip's grasp and raced to the man ahead of Jack. Chip followed in pursuit, but by the time he reached Blaze the dog was walking all over the man and licking his face. The boys had a hard time dragging Blaze off, but after Chip gave him a few shoves, the dog finally got the idea that they wanted him to stay away.

"You think it's okay to move him?" Chip said, squatting down beside his brother.

Jack lifted the man to a sitting position, and the boys could see that he was younger than they had thought—about nineteen, just a couple of years older than Jack. His shoulders and face were badly sunburned. Judging by the whiteness of the rest of his body, the boys guessed that he did not spend much time outdoors.

His appearance contrasted sharply with the tanned appearance of both Jack and Chip. The sun had bleached Chip's blond hair. Jack's freckled face and short reddish-brown hair personified ruddy good health.

"The way it looked," Jack said, "he just passed out."

"See how he's burned. Maybe he got too much sun all at once. We've got to do something. But—but what?"

Music began drifting lazily but distinctly across the wide bay.

"That must be coming from the club where Dad's taking pictures," Chip said.

"Run up to the house, Chip. One of the guests might be a doctor. I'll stay here. But get going! Hurry!"

Chip arose quickly. Blaze had been watching quietly from a distance. Now he started to bark.

Chip began running for the house, with Blaze barking and prancing around him. Jack called Chip's name, and when his brother turned around, he shouted, "Come back here! Hurry!"

Chip rushed back. The young man had made it to his feet, but he was very unsteady.

"You sure you're all right?" Jack asked him.

The fellow nodded, but with difficulty. He raised his head for a moment, then let it drop.

When Jack and Chip tried to take his arms to help him, he shrugged them off. He staggered away from them, up the slope of the lawn, while the boys stood helplessly watching him. Blaze remained behind, too. He had something in his mouth, worrying it with violent shakes of his head.

"What's he got?" Jack asked curiously.

"Don't expect him to tell you," Chip answered. He straddled Blaze and tugged at the object in the dog's mouth. "You couldn't talk either if you had this thing in your—"

"It's a foot flipper, isn't it?" Jack interrupted.

"How did you know?"

"Don't sound so surprised. I just picked up its mate."

"Stop whining, Blaze," Chip told the Dalmatian. "You're not going to get me to give this back to you." Holding the swim fin high in the air, he passed it to Jack. Then he told his brother excitedly, "I just thought of something. You know why that guy passed out? He must have been diving a lot. And that on top of all his sunburn could have. . . ." Chip didn't finish.

"Yeah. Sure," Jack answered as they walked slowly back toward the guesthouse. Blaze moved along beside them, his eyes on the fins which Jack was now carrying. "But what I'm curious about," Jack continued, "is why he acted the way he did. Didn't he seem scared to you?"

"He acted peculiar," Chip admitted. "That's for sure."

"It's tough," Jack murmured.

"Yeah. I know what you mean. Seeing a fellow scared is—"

"Chip, that's not what I meant. We're leaving tomorrow. So there's not much chance we'll ever find out what's wrong with him."

The boys stopped at the door and looked back across the lawn. The orange in the sky had lost its brilliance, but the music coming across the water was still very clear. Blaze found a tennis ball and started chewing on it.

When the boys entered the guesthouse, the card players were playing in the same quiet, serious way they were when the boys had left.

"Hey, the Ping-Pong table's not being used!" Chip exclaimed in surprise. "Now's our chance, Jack!"

"Just hold onto the table." Jack went toward the registration desk with the swim fins in his hand. "I might as well turn these things in now."

Jack placed the fins on the desk as he waited for the clerk to appear.

"Come on," Chip called. "We've finally got the table, so how about playing?" He stood at one end of the table and pretended to be returning a ball in play, using vicious swipes and unreturnable overhand slams.

To call the clerk, Jack struck the bell on the desk with the palm of his hand. A knocking sounded in the office behind the desk.

"Come here, Chip," Jack said.

Because Jack sounded both puzzled and startled, Chip headed for the registration desk. By this time Jack had already hurried through the little gate at the side of the desk. He stopped and held the gate open for Chip.

"Don't start asking me questions," Jack said before Chip could speak. "Just come on."

The door to the office was open. The boys went in and looked around. It was plain that no one was there.

"May I ask *one* question?" Chip said, then laughed. "I mean, besides the one I just asked."

Jack held up his hand. *"Shhh!"* he whispered.

As the boys stood motionless they heard a knocking sound. It came from the far end of the office, from an alcove off to the right. The boys hurried to the spot.

There they found a gray-haired woman lying on the floor. Though she was tied and gagged, her blue eyes lit up when she saw the boys. Without a word, Jack got down on one side of her and Chip on the other. Chip worked at untying the rope at her wrists, while Jack removed the gag from her mouth, then loosened the bindings on her ankles.

The woman's first words were "To think that such a thing would happen to me." She cleared her throat and rubbed the corners of her mouth. "You're the Power boys. Jack. Chip. I know." She was plainly proud of her knowledge. "Your father's the photographer. And you're in room five."

"Are you all right?" Jack asked anxiously.

"Oh, yes, yes, of course." As though to prove she was all right, she rose quickly to her feet. She was a small woman with rosy cheeks and very blue eyes. Her gray hair was cut short. The quick way she moved and spoke made her seem young.

"To be tied up and gagged! I can't get over it. I thought that was only done in old movies. And you came to the rescue. That was like one of those movies, too. Oh, I should introduce myself. Mrs. Alice Wilson. I'm Mrs. Alice Wilson. Would you," she said, suddenly sober, "would you please not say a word of this to anyone?"

"Golly," Chip said, "what happened?"

The woman glanced in the direction of the safe, which rested against one wall of the alcove. The safe's door had been practically torn off.

"Wow!" Chip exclaimed.

"A rip job," Jack said, identifying the technique the burglar had used.

"You mean you're not going to call the police?" Chip asked in amazement. "Or whatever police are called in Bermuda."

"Remember the favor I asked of you," Mrs. Wilson said, picking up a piece of rope.

"Something like this should be reported, it seems to me," Jack said slowly.

Chip nodded his agreement.

Mrs. Wilson picked up two more pieces of rope, mechanically tidying up. She looked at Jack and Chip for a moment without saying anything. Then she said positively, "Boys, nothing was stolen. Nothing. Absolutely nothing."

"How do you know?" Chip asked.

"He tied my mouth but not my eyes," Mrs. Wilson answered. She moved quickly to the mangled door. "I saw that he looked and looked, then didn't take a thing. Such inefficiency. Especially in the age of computers, atoms, and all the rest."

The boys stared in amazement at the ripped-open safe.

"What was he after?" Jack asked. "You have any idea?"

"See all these valuables with tags on them?" Mrs. Wilson's hand gestured to indicate them all. "They belong to the guests. They're left here for safekeeping."

"And this burglar just left them all?" Chip asked, puzzled.

"I told you," Mrs. Wilson said, "he didn't take a thing."

"But—but shouldn't this be reported?" Jack asked.

Mrs. Wilson shook her head. She took a large cloth from a desk drawer and threw it over the safe. The boys helped her straighten the cloth so that it covered the safe completely.

"I don't want anyone to see the safe in its present condition," she said. "Even an attempted robbery would give my guesthouse a bad name. And there's so much competition these days. Now do you understand why I don't want this to be reported?"

"We won't say anything," Jack said.

Chip shook his head in agreement.

The boys left, but they stopped just outside of their room.

"Only one conclusion you can come to," Jack said.

"About why she won't go to the cops?"

"This burglar was after a special thing that he thought one of the guests had," Jack continued. "And either the guest didn't have this thing to start with, or he's got it and didn't check it at the office."

"Golly. But wouldn't you think he'd have grabbed all that other stuff? A regular burglar would have."

"What are you saying, Chip? That he's an amateur? Why—why you saw the job he did on that safe."

"Yeah. Sure. But I still don't see why he'd—"

"Hey!" Jack interrupted. "I just thought of something. That burglar may have been hired to get one thing. Maybe he was told not to touch anything else."

"So why are you all excited?" Chip asked.

"He didn't find what he was after in the safe. That means the guest didn't check it at the office. And if he didn't do that, the thing is probably in his room. And assuming this burglar's got a brain, his next move would be—"

"Yeah." Chip's eyes were wide with excitement. "He'd go to this guy's room."

"But we don't know what room that would be, because we don't know who the guest is. . . ."

Jack's voice trailed off thoughtfully. As the boys stood there in the silence they could hear the music coming over the bay from the club where their father was taking pictures. Suddenly they heard a sound coming from their room.

They stared at one another in surprise.

"Somebody's in *our* room!" Chip gasped. "Is it the burglar—do you think?"

2 *Underwater Assignment*

"But Dad hasn't got what the burglar is after," Jack whispered.

They remained motionless, listening. Someone was obviously walking around in the room.

"Look, Chip," Jack said, suddenly decisive. "You go outside, in case he leaves by the window. I'll give you a little time to position yourself. Then I'll open the door and—"

"How about getting some guests to help?"

Jack shook his head.

"But, Jack, what are we going to use for protection?" Chip asked. "I'm not in the mood to get clobbered."

"You heard Mrs. Wilson. She wants to keep this all quiet. It would wreck her business—if it got out a burglar was on the loose here."

"Where's Blaze?" Chip asked. Then, suddenly, excitedly, he put his ear flat to the panel of the door. After a few seconds of listening, he came away from the door saying, "I was right. I did hear claws scraping on the floor. Whoever is in there has got Blaze for company."

"Could it be Dad? But the music over at the club is still playing."

The boys quickly pushed open the door.

Blaze was stretched out full length on the floor. He thumped his tail on the floor in mild greeting. There was nothing unusual going on in this room, the boys realized.

"Where have you two been?" Mr. Power asked, emerging from the bathroom which served as a darkroom. He had freshly developed prints in his hand. He was as tall as Jack, but heavier. His hair was black, with premature gray in it.

The boys blinked in astonishment.

"Did you shoot the pictures you wanted?" Jack asked his father.

"Of course I got the pictures. Why do you sound so surprised?"

"Well, the music's still going full blast across the bay and we thought—"

"What? That I was going to stick around and dance? I seem to have gotten more of a welcome from Blaze than I'm getting from you."

Mr. Power put the prints beside the others spread on the bed. As he headed back to his improvised darkroom, he stopped suddenly.

"Did something happen while I was gone?" he asked, studying both his sons suspiciously.

Chip glanced at Jack as if he didn't know how he should answer that.

Jack laughed. "I'll tell you what happened, Dad. There was some terrific action out on the porch. One of the card players moved. Actually. He stood up and stretched."

"That's right," Chip said solemnly. "No kidding."

Mr. Powers smiled, but his thoughts were obviously

not on what his sons were saying.

"What's the matter, Dad?" Jack asked.

Mr. Power walked over to the bed where the prints lay. "Come here, boys," he said, making a beckoning gesture.

The prints were of typical Bermuda scenes: a sail-boat race, the pastel pink limestone houses, the bicycle riders. . . . Mr. Power was doing a picture story for the Caribbean Association which was trying to counter-act the impression that the Caribbean, because of politi-cal unrest, wasn't safe for tourists. Bermuda and the Bahamas were included.

"I know you've found it quiet around here . . ." Mr. Power began finally.

Chip's eyes lit up excitedly. "Are we going to get to go with you after all?"

Mr. Power held up his hand. "I'm afraid not, Chip," he said. "After the Bahamas, I'm going to be hopping from island to island. You and Jack—and especially Blaze—would complicate the travel arrangements. I've told you all this time and again."

"Couldn't you see Dad was trying to tell us something

—something new?" Jack said to Chip. "Why did you have to interrupt him?"

Mr. Power was silent for a long moment. He avoided the boys' eyes by looking down at the prints on the bed. "There's a lot of natural beauty here," he said. "But it is quiet," he conceded.

"Golly, Dad," Jack said, "you sound like you're thinking of having us remain in Bermuda because it's so dead."

Chip stared hard at Jack, thinking of all that had just happened. His forehead was furrowed in the attempt to understand what Jack was up to. Then, to back up his brother, he said quickly, "That's right, Dad. We don't object to something beautiful. It's just that there's nothing much exciting—"

"Yes, yes, I know," Mr. Power broke in on Chip. "It's the lack of excitement that bothers you. Well, I might as well tell you. I've decided that you shouldn't go back to New York. Papers every day are full of the crime that's going on. And there's nothing like that here."

"But we're not exactly kids," Jack protested. "I'm not

ten, you know. I'm seventeen."

"When you went to California that time," Chip put in, "we stayed in New York by ourselves and we made out."

Mr. Power nodded. "I know that, Chip. But maybe this time—you wouldn't make out. So I want you to stay here. And that's definite. Understand?"

Chip shrugged. "Okay, Dad, okay."

Jack nodded his head silently, thoughtfully.

When the boys went to the bathroom to brush their teeth and get ready for bed, Jack turned a lavatory faucet on full force.

"I don't want Dad to hear us talking," he explained in a whisper to Chip. "If he knew what was happening here, he certainly wouldn't want us to stay."

A rapping started on the door. "Don't upset anything!" Mr. Power shouted in to them.

"We won't!" Jack yelled back.

"There's acetic acid in there."

Jack turned the water down. "We're not touching it. Don't worry," he yelled. Then he turned on the water again. "Chip, we've got to convince him it's dead here."

The boys stood silently for a moment in the bathroom, which was crowded with photographic equipment.

Drawing as close as he could to Jack, Chip whispered, "You don't really want to go back to New York, do you?"

"No. It's not only that burglary that's got me curious," Jack answered. He turned the water off and back on again a few times to give his father the impression that they were washing up. "I'm also curious," he went on, "about that sunburned guy who passed out on the lawn. Now look, Chip, we've got to be careful. We don't want Dad talking to Mrs. Wilson. He'll know pretty fast we're trying to figure out who cracked open her safe. Another thing, let's not put it on too thick that we want to go to New York. Instead of making Dad more determined than ever that we stay here, he's liable to give in and let us go."

Chip shook his head. He knew it was because their mother wasn't alive that their father felt overly responsible for them. "He won't change his mind," Chip said with certainty.

The rapping on the door sounded again. "Boys!" Mr.

Power called. "Would you hurry up? I've something to tell you!"

Jack turned the water off. "Okay, Dad!" he called. He folded his arms, a worried expression on his freckled face. "What did that sound like to you?" he whispered to Chip. "Golly, have we changed his mind already?"

"Don't worry," Chip whispered. "He's not giving in. He meant what he said. He doesn't want us going to New York."

Mr. Power stood in the middle of the living room, obviously waiting for them. "Boys," he began as soon as they stepped out of the bathroom, "I don't want to be hard on you. . . ."

Jack and Chip exchanged glances. The set of Jack's tightened lips seemed to say, "What'd I tell you?"

"I know you're afraid of being bored here," Mr. Power went on. "So I've thought of something."

Jack and Chip glanced at one another again, this time puzzled and uncertain.

"I want you to take some underwater pictures for me," Mr. Power said. "How does that strike you?"

"Wow!" Chip exclaimed. "You want *us* to?"

"But you're not to go too deep or take a lot of chances."

"That's great, Dad," Chip said, emphasizing each word.

"It sure is," Jack agreed.

"Oh, it's great all right," Mr. Power said with a parent's sarcasm. "But it's also dangerous. Here I am canceling the New York trip, but giving you something instead that's—"

"We'll be careful, Dad," Jack said.

"Remember. Neither one of you is *ever* to dive alone."

"Of course not," Chip said.

"Will you stop worrying, Dad?" Jack added patiently.

"And be careful not to get away from the boat you're diving from," Mr. Power reminded them.

Jack laughed. "You forgot something, Dad. To tell us not to let the boat get away from us."

"I just wonder," the boys' father mused grimly, "if I'm doing the right thing."

3 *"A Bad Omen"*

"Golly, Dad," Chip said, "you're doing the right thing."

Mr. Power snapped his fingers as an idea occurred to him. He rushed off to the phone. As he dialed he told his sons, "If I can make reservations on a night flight, why stick around another day? I'll be able to get to the Bahamas—"

He didn't finish. The party he was calling had come on the wire.

"It's all set," he told the boys as he hung up. He studied his wristwatch. "The one o'clock plane from Kindley Field. I don't have an awful lot of time."

"You can make it," Chip said in an offhand way. "We'll help you pack."

Mr. Power and his sons began to rush around. Suitcases were pulled out and opened. As he hurried to assemble his equipment in the bathroom, Mr. Power stopped suddenly.

"I've overlooked something important," Mr. Power said, obviously irritated with himself. "You may not be able to go on staying here. They've probably already reserved this room for someone, since you were due to leave for New York tomorrow."

"I doubt that," Chip said.

"Well, I want to be sure you're settled before I take off."

"Don't worry, Dad." Jack tried to turn his father around. "Go on, take care of your equipment."

"It'll just take me a minute to check," Mr. Power said.

Jack maintained his hold on his father. "We can handle it, Dad. You're pressed for time. You said so yourself."

Mr. Power appeared to weaken. "All right," he said.

"But I want you to go to the desk clerk right now."

"Okay, Dad," Jack agreed, starting off.

"I'll go with him," Chip said.

Just outside the door, the boys stopped.

"Listen, Chip," Jack said, "we want to be sure Dad doesn't get a chance to talk to Mrs. Wilson before he takes off."

Chip nodded. "That's why you said you'd check with her. Right?"

"Well, I know she wouldn't be able to keep from telling him how we untied her—and all the rest."

Chip laughed. "Maybe we're heroes."

They started walking toward the registration desk.

"I wonder how long we've been heroes without knowing it," Chip said.

Jack stopped. "Come on, Chip. Knock it off. What I've been trying to tell you is this: We don't want Dad finding out before he leaves that there's crime around here, too."

"He must know New York's not the only place."

Jack made no further comment. When they reached the registration desk, they found that there was no one behind it. The light had been turned out over the Ping-Pong table. Darkness had also claimed the screened porch, routing the card players.

"Isn't this where we came in?" Chip said. "Don't tell me Mrs. Wilson's tied up again!"

"Shhh!"

"Did you hear something?" Chip asked.

Jack didn't answer. He held himself perfectly still, listening. Chip also strained to hear.

"You've got me over a barrel," a man's voice said.

Jack's eyes lit up with surprise and excitement.

"You think she's caught the crook?" Chip asked hoarsely.

"Wait a second," Jack said, preparing to listen again.

Impulsively Chip headed for the office on the run. Jack rushed after him, whispering his name with urgency in an attempt to stop him.

They both came to a stop at the opened door of the office. Facing Mrs. Wilson stood the honeymoon couple who always monopolized the Ping-Pong table.

When she noticed them in the doorway Mrs. Wilson beckoned to Jack and Chip and introduced them, adding that they were the ones who had found her bound hand and foot after the robbery.

"Mr. Fallone," she went on, "is an officer on the police force in the States—in Peoria. It is in Peoria, isn't it?"

Mr. Fallone nodded.

"And Mary's his bride. They're leaving in the morning. And I thought that before they went I'd ask Mr. Fallone about—you know, my little trouble."

"As I was saying, ma'm, this is a felony." Mr. Fallone's brow was furrowed over the seriousness of the crime. "A B-E job. Breaking-and-entering, that's what it is."

"He thinks I should report it," Mrs. Wilson told Jack and Chip.

Mary Fallone looked with pride at her brand-new husband. She was holding one of his hands with both of hers.

And Mr. Fallone was showing off for all he was worth before his bride. "A misdemeanor," he said solemnly, "that's something else again."

"That rip job on the safe was done by a pro, wouldn't

you say?" Jack asked Mr. Fallone.

The question seemed to catch Mr. Fallone unawares, but he quickly recovered and said, "Oh, yes," with great authority.

"You think it might have been an inside job?" Jack asked.

"No." Mr. Fallone shook his head. "Oh, no."

Mrs. Fallone beamed because her husband was so masterful, so sure of himself.

"You're speaking another language," Mrs. Wilson said reprovingly to Jack. "By inside job, do you mean that one of my guests did it?"

Mr. Fallone nodded importantly. "Right," he announced, before Jack could answer. "That's the meaning of an inside job."

"What makes you so sure?" Jack asked Mr. Fallone. "I mean, that it wasn't done by somebody—"

"Why, Jack," Mrs. Wilson cut in, outraged, "I don't have a criminal clientele."

"Right." Mr. Fallone nodded more vigorously. "Right. Exactly. Nine tenths of police work is being able to size people up."

"Vinnie is an instructor in the police academy in Peoria," Mrs. Fallone told the group proudly.

Mr. and Mrs. Fallone beamed at one another.

Chip looked away in disgust; he couldn't take any more of this. Suddenly he spotted his father pacing at the registration desk.

"Hey, Jack!" Chip headed for the door. "Dad's out there!"

"Where have you been?" Mr. Power asked Jack and Chip impatiently, as they came rushing up to him.

"Oh," Chip muttered, flustered as well as out of breath. "Huh, uh. . . ."

"Have you arranged to stay on here?"

"Sure thing, Dad," Jack said in relief.

"Good! Great! I already have my things in a cab." As he moved with the boys toward the door a horn outside gave a few quick beeps. "That's the cabbie. He wants to be sure I make my plane. There's a twenty-mile speed limit here, you know."

"Dad, how about our going to the airport with you?" Chip asked.

"Oh, I wish you could," Mr. Power said. "But just

wait, you'll see why you can't."

The cab was a compact, and a small one at that. Even though it was dark outside, it was plain that luggage and equipment filled the rear of the cab. The end of a tripod protruded from a window.

Before getting in beside the driver, Mr. Power gave Jack money for any incidental expenses the boys might have while he was away. He shook hands with them as he got into the cab.

As the cab started off, Mr. Power shouted out to them, "Oh, yes! The underwater camera's on your bed! Check the housing. . . ."

Jack waved. But Chip ran after the car, keeping pace with it down the winding drive.

"I'll get some good pictures for you!" Chip yelled to his father.

Mr. Power shouted something about not doing anything reckless. Before he could finish, the cab came to a straightaway and pulled away from Chip.

Chip tripped over himself in coming to a stop. As he got to his feet, Jack came up at a trot. "What happened to you?" he asked.

"You know why I fell?" Chip said, irritated by his brother's question. "You told Dad we were all set here. I was thinking of that and the next thing I knew I went flat on my face."

"You okay?"

"Sure," Chip said, limping toward the guesthouse with Jack. "Outside of a broken arm and— It's funny. The second Dad leaves, bang—down I go!"

"What do you mean? That this is a bad omen?"

"Yeah," Chip said. "Maybe that's what I do mean."

When they entered the guesthouse Mrs. Wilson was just dimming the light over the registration desk. She noticed right away that Chip was limping.

"What's wrong?" she asked with concern. "Did you fall?" She came quickly toward them.

Jack laughed. "It's your fault, Mrs. Wilson."

"My fault?" The woman looked bewildered.

"You see, we're not leaving Bermuda tomorrow, the way we had planned."

"Don't pay attention to him," Chip said hastily.

"My brother was so worried you'd kick us out," Jack went on, "that he fell. He told me so himself."

"Hmmm," Mrs. Wilson said thoughtfully. "Your room is taken. People from Boston have a reservation for that room. A couple and their daughter. But," she continued, "number eight was vacated today. It's smaller and—"

"That's okay," Chip said quickly.

"We don't mind if it's smaller," Jack echoed.

"And it doesn't have a view of the ocean," Mrs. Wilson warned them. "Come. I'll show it to you. Then you can decide."

The boys approved of the new room as soon as they entered it. Blaze did, too, by immediately dropping full length on a rug. When Mrs. Wilson saw how their father had cluttered up the other room in the course of his hurried departure, she insisted that they move into their new room immediately.

"It's a small enough courtesy," she said, "after what you two have done for me." She looked closely at Jack. "It's a crime, Jack, that you should have that magnificent red hair." She laughed. "It should be mine."

After the boys went to bed Chip began to wonder out loud if there was something wrong with the housing of the underwater camera. "All Dad said was to check it," he mused.

"We won't even be able to do that," Jack said, "if we don't get some sleep."

"Maybe it's being in this new room," Chip continued. "I don't feel too much like sleeping."

"Okay," Jack said. "But how about letting me sleep?"

"It's funny. I mean, that being in this different room—"

"Go to sleep." Jack's voice was sharp.

"—should affect me," Chip finished, "and not you."

"Good night, Chip."

"Maybe it's because I don't think that cop from Peoria knows what he's talking about. Any guest here might be a crook. You can't tell if a guy's honest or not by the way he looks."

Jack flopped around noisily, letting his brother know that he wanted no more conversation.

Soon both boys were asleep. They didn't hear or see the man who slowly and carefully removed the screen on the window.

4 *"X Marks the Spot...."*

When the man had one leg over the windowsill he bent a little to one side and raised his other leg slowly and carefully. He remained motionless on the window-sill, making sure the coast was clear before he made another move.

Chip woke up. His arm hurt. He opened his eyes lazily, hoping his arm wouldn't keep him awake all night. As he was about to move the injured arm to a more comfortable position, he saw the shadowy figure framed in the window.

Chip lay perfectly still. The only sound was the regular rhythm of Jack's breathing. He remembered what his father had once said about burglars.

"It's not a good idea to raise a racket if you hear a burglar," his father had warned. "Let him take what he wants and go. Burglars are usually armed. If you interfere with them, they're liable to shoot. . . ."

The silhouette in the window stood up. It waited, not making another movement until it was sure it was unnoticed.

Jack awoke. He didn't jump up, startled, but he was aware of the sudden pounding of his heart. When he spotted the silhouette framed in the window he felt certain that the awareness of a stranger in the room had awakened him. His next thought was what his father had said about the danger of disturbing a burglar at work. He hoped Chip didn't wake up—and do something foolish.

Both Jack and Chip lay motionless, scarcely daring to breathe.

The dark figure took a step, slowly and carefully. Then another.

The boys—their eyes wide, staring into the darkness of the room—knew the man was moving from the window toward the foot of the bed.

Another step. Then a sudden outcry caused Jack and Chip to spring up in bed, startled and confused. The outcry came from Blaze, who was yelping and whining in pain. An overturned chair added to the confusion as the intruder made a headlong rush to escape out the window.

Because they were not familiar with the new room, the boys fumbled frantically before Jack found the light switch. Blaze was still whining, his body close to the floor. He looked up pleadingly at the boys.

Chip picked up the overturned chair. He dropped to one knee and ran his hand comfortingly from Blaze's head down his back. "That's all right," he said soothingly. "Good boy, good boy. . . ."

Jack rushed to the window and looked out into the darkness.

"Do you think it was the same crook?" Chip asked, continuing to stroke Blaze.

Jack turned from the window and looked about the room. "Wonder if he swiped anything," he mused.

Chip arose and went limping to the closet. He looked

on the shelf. "The camera's here!" he exclaimed happily. "Am I glad he didn't take this!" Chip picked up the 16 mm. Kolex movie camera with a Kolex underwater housing, as though to convince himself that it really hadn't been stolen. "Is anything missing?"

Jack didn't answer.

"What's that?" Chip asked, seeing Jack pick up something from the floor.

"It's not ours." Jack looked down at the long roll of paper which lay across the palms of his hands. "And I didn't see it around when we went to bed. But there it was, right on the floor, near the bed. I'm surprised we didn't step on it when we were rushing around."

Chip quickly put the camera back on the closet shelf and hurried over to Jack.

"This is some burglar," Chip said. "He rips off a safe door and doesn't take anything. And this time, not only doesn't he take anything, but he leaves this, this—whatever it is."

Jack was taking the rubber band off the roll. "They always roll up blueprints this way," he said knowingly.

"Yeah, I know. And diplomas, too."

Jack started to unroll the paper. Because of its size, he found it was easier unrolling it on the bed. It took the hands of both boys to hold down the paper's corners.

"It's a map," Chip said disappointedly.

"No. It's a navigation chart." Jack peered closely at one corner of the chart. "It's of the North Atlantic. The islands around here. Maybe this thing was on the floor last night—when we took over the room. Could be we just didn't see it."

"I know. How about the people who were in the room before us? Maybe they forgot it."

Blaze was up on his feet now. He looked back at his tail and whined a little.

Jack and Chip let go of the chart, and it rolled up on its own.

"How are you, Blaze?" Chip asked cheerily. "I thought he had his paw stepped on, didn't you, Jack? But it looks like it was his tail."

Jack scratched his head. "What would have happened if that guy hadn't stepped on Blaze's tail?"

Chip shrugged. "You would have gone on sleeping, for one thing, and—"

"You mean *you* would have," Jack objected. "I was wide awake."

After a little more talk, the boys realized they had both been awake and that each had thought the other was asleep.

"You know how I figure it?" Chip said. "This guy just breaks into places for kicks. If he wanted to swipe stuff, he could have helped himself to all the valuables in Mrs. Wilson's safe. But he doesn't. He passes it all up to come in here. And outside of Dad's camera, what have we got worth taking?"

After they turned off the lights and crawled back in bed, Jack said, "No point in telling Mrs. Wilson about this. It would just make her feel bad."

"Wonder what that cop from Peoria would say about this," Chip mused. "Oh, no. I wouldn't tell Mrs. Wilson. She'd feel awful, knowing this sort of thing was happening in her guesthouse."

"Let's go to sleep," Jack said. Then a thought occurred to him. "You know what we ought to do tomorrow? Check on everybody who's staying here."

"How?" Chip asked. "What kind of checking?"

Instead of answering Chip, Jack got out of bed, turned on the light, and said, "I want to take another look at that chart."

"Another look!" Chip exclaimed. "Why?"

"When I said 'check' just now"—Jack was unrolling the map on the bed as he spoke—"something clicked in my head." He studied the chart. "Yeah," he said excitedly. "Sure enough, here it is. It's not a check mark. It's an X. When I saw it before, it didn't register."

Chip crawled across the bed. "What are you talking about?" he asked, looking down at the chart.

Jack put his finger on the chart. "See this in red ink?"

"I probably saw it before. What about it?"

"Did you ever hear of X marking the spot?"

"Yeah, sure."

"This could be a rendezvous spot," Jack said as he rolled up the map. Chip sat motionless in the middle of the bed, waiting for Jack to go on. "Don't you understand?"

Chip shook his head.

"Why, this is the first step in a plot," Jack explained. "We've got the chart marked with the red X. Now all we have to do is wait for whoever broke in to make the next move."

"What?" Chip said, aghast. "You're dreaming. You dreamed all that up."

"Oh, no, I didn't," Jack disagreed. "There's only one thing that doesn't fit."

Chip got under the covers. "How about turning off the lights?" he said irritably. "I wouldn't mind doing some dreaming myself."

"Did the same guy break into Mrs. Wilson's safe and into our room?" Jack asked himself. "If he did, what was he after in the safe?"

Chip turned over on his side. He was as tired now as Jack had been earlier.

"I'm also wondering," Jack went on, "when we'll be contacted next."

Just then Blaze growled—a low, challenging growl.

Chip scrambled out from under the covers, then remained motionless.

"Could this be it?" Jack whispered ominously.

As though in answer, Blaze moved toward the door, growling threateningly.

5 *Strange Encounter*

"Go on," Chip mouthed. "Open the door."

"I can't!" Jack exclaimed in a tense whisper. "Blaze will go charging out! And people are sleeping."

"All right," Chip said, grabbing Blaze's collar. "Go ahead and open it now. I'm holding him. My arm seems to be okay."

Finally Jack opened the door.

The man standing there laughed in embarrassment. "I was just about to knock," he said. The white shirt he wore contrasted strongly with his deep tan. He held several blankets. "Some blankets for you," he said as he handed them over to Jack. "I hope I didn't wake you."

He backed away, muttering apologetically.

As soon as Jack closed the door, Chip let go of Blaze.

"What do you think that was all about?" Chip asked in amazement.

Jack dropped the blankets on the bed. "The guy brought us blankets. What else?"

Chip shrugged doubtfully.

"Hotels and places like this usually give you blankets," Jack continued. "And because we moved into a new room. . . ."

"I don't know." Chip went around the foot of the bed and started getting under the covers. He sounded dubious. "What makes me suspicious is the way Blaze acted. He usually can tell a good guy from a bad guy."

"Forget it," Jack said.

But when they were both back in bed, and the lights were out, Jack brought up the subject again.

"You're forgetting that Blaze just had his tail stepped on," Jack said. "What's more, he was sleeping when it happened."

"But when Blaze growls that way. . . ."

"You're on edge," Jack accused.

"Not any more than you are," Chip objected.

"So we're both on edge. And we both have to be careful not to go imagining a lot of things."

While Chip was thinking of a way to answer Jack he fell asleep.

When he awoke, it was bright daylight. Jack sat hunched over the camera on the drop-leaf desk.

"How is it?" Chip asked. "Is it okay?"

"Oh, you're awake, huh?" Jack said, straightening and looking over at Chip. "I thought of something."

"Oh, yeah?"

"I don't mean about the camera. Not exactly about the camera. My idea is to—"

"Jack," Chip said, getting out of bed, "you're not making any sense."

"Look, Chip." Jack stood up. He ran his hand through his close-cropped red hair. "It would be interesting, wouldn't it, to catch this crook?"

"You were just talking about the camera, weren't you?"

"Let's assume," Jack went on, as though Chip hadn't spoken, "that the crook's one of the guests. So what we've got to do is get to know the people. Talk to them."

"We talked to that cop from Peoria last night. Say, what if he's just posing as a cop?" Chip brightened at the thought.

Jack looked pained.

"Well, crooks have been known to dress up like cops and—"

"Yeah. Yeah, I know," Jack said, nodding. "I've seen those movies. But—but will you listen to the scheme I've got?" Then he explained that by carrying their camera around, they could draw people into conversation about photography. And from there the people could be led into talk about other things.

The boys were on their way to have breakfast when Jack suddenly stopped at the dining-room entrance. "Let's not go in right away," he said. He turned and went outside.

Chip went along reluctantly. "Aren't you hungry?" he complained. "I am. I'd like something to eat."

Jack didn't say anything. He didn't stop until he was some distance from the pastel pink guesthouse. Off in the distance the water of the bay sparkled in the bright sun, creating a peaceful scene.

"I didn't want to talk in there," Jack said, keeping his voice low.

"Why?" Chip asked curiously. "What gives?"

"Let's walk. Somebody might be watching. Our standing here talking would look suspicious."

"Okay," Chip agreed. "But we're heading back to the dining room. I'm hungry. What was that about somebody watching us?"

They stopped again before reaching the house. Jack explained that he had suddenly decided that what had happened must be more than a simple case of burglary. "And if we could somehow get the crook to believe we're crooked, too. . . ."

"He'd really talk then, you mean?" Chip interrupted eagerly.

"Not only that," Jack said. "He might even ask us to join up with him. And if that happened—"

A man and a woman coming out of the house caused Jack to break off. They were laughing and talking about something that obviously struck them as being very funny. Both of them wore white shorts.

"Dad's in the Bahamas now." Jack pointed in the direction of the bay, for the benefit of the man and woman. "That's where those islands are. South, southwest of here."

As soon as the couple had passed, Chip said, "Dad wouldn't go for this at all. Remember that, Jack. If we get mixed up with crooks and they find out we're honest, they're not going to like it. They might even get violent."

Jack reassured Chip, then they went in to have breakfast. They went on into the dining room, to find only one table filled. All the others were set, but empty. The boys sat down at the first table they came to.

They had finished orange juice and cold cereal and were just starting on their bacon and eggs when the sunburned fellow who had passed out the night before came into the dining room. Just as the boys looked up, he looked over in their direction. He glanced away quickly. Jack and Chip saw the waiter direct him to the table where the boys sat. Instead of following his direction, however, the fellow said something to the waiter in low tones. The waiter then led the way to another table near the windows.

"I almost forgot about him," Jack muttered.

"What's he got against us?" Chip asked. "Why wouldn't he want to sit with us?"

"Maybe because we saw him collapse in a heap last night," Jack suggested.

After breakfast the boys wandered about outside. Chip carried the movie camera faithfully. It drew a few glances, but no comments.

Four elderly women played croquet silently on the side lawn. The only sound was the click of the mallets against the wooden balls. The boys watched two men and two women start for Hamilton on their rented English bikes. Everything was peaceful. The only thing that suggested crime was the policeman from Peoria, Illinois, who was departing with his bride. In saying good-bye, Mrs. Wilson sauntered out to a cab with them.

Jack and Chip arose from the grass where they had been sitting and observing the leisurely activity around the guesthouse.

"What we going to do now?" Chip asked. "In New York there'd be plenty to do."

"Dad was against our going, remember?"

"Yeah. And I remember something else. By saying we wanted to go to New York, we made sure he'd say we were staying right here in Bermuda."

"How about those underwater shots?" Jack suggested. "You were anxious to take them."

"Yeah," Chip admitted. "I guess I am."

"Well, you certainly got excited when Dad made the offer."

As they started toward their room to gather the equipment someone called to them.

It was the sunburned fellow. Cold cream covered the ridge of his red nose. A towel protected his shoulders. He was thin, with curly brown hair.

"Can I talk to you for a minute?" he said nervously. He went on to apologize for not having sat with them at breakfast. His only reason was that he had wanted to sit near the window, he declared. "But I realized right away," he went on, "that it must have looked as if I was snubbing you. Believe me, I wasn't."

Chip smiled. "We should have picked a table near the window ourselves. The scenery is beautiful around here."

After that, Jack and Chip introduced themselves. The sunburned fellow's name was Bob Jillman. He shook hands with the boys. Then there was a moment of embarrassed silence.

"That's a nice camera you have there," Bob said, obviously ill at ease.

"We've got to do a little adjusting on it," Jack said.

"Mrs. Wilson told me your father's a photographer," Bob Jillman said. "He does underwater work. Do you?"

Jack and Chip exchanged glances. It was apparent they were both thinking the same thing: Why would this guy be questioning Mrs. Wilson about them?

"We're going to take some pictures," Jack answered finally. "Before we do, I want to be sure of just how much pressure the housing on this camera can stand."

"That means you dive, huh?" Bob asked, more nervous now than ever.

Both Jack and Chip nodded. Another heavy silence followed.

Impulsively Chip said what he was thinking. "It sounds," he said, "like you're leading up to something. Am I right?"

The instant he spoke, Chip wished he hadn't.

Bob took a deep breath. He ran his tongue over his lips. He had been leading up to something, there wasn't any question about that.

The boys waited expectantly. They had been talking about making contact with the burglar. Was Bob Jillman the contact they had been hoping for?

6 *Table Talk*

"You were right," Bob said to Chip finally.

Jack and Chip waited for him to go on.

Bob moistened his lips again. "You said you dive. And I was wondering. . . ."

To cover the uncomfortable pause that followed, Jack said, "What do you want us to do? Dive for something?"

Bob shook his head. "No, oh, no," he protested. "I have to do the diving. But I have to learn how. And I was wondering if I could get you to teach me."

It had all come out in such an unexpected rush that Jack and Chip were left speechless.

"I'd pay for the lessons, of course," Bob added quickly.

"That's all well and good, Bob," Jack said. "We could do it, I guess, but—"

"Well?" Bob's grip tensed on the towel over his shoulders. "Will you?"

"You said you'd pay—"

"Sure," Bob said eagerly. "Sure."

"The thing is," Jack went on, "you'd do a lot better, for your money, going to a regular diving school. There are a lot of 'em around."

"There sure are," Chip chimed in.

Bob squirmed nervously. "I must learn—in a hurry," he said, looking down at his feet.

"Have you done any diving?" Jack asked.

Bob's head snapped up. "Why all the questions?" he demanded. "Do you want to teach me or don't you?"

"It's not that, Bob. If you haven't done any diving, you're not going to learn in a hurry."

"What's the rush, anyway?" Chip asked.

There was no answer. Bob glared at the two boys for a moment and then marched away.

The boys stood looking at Bob's sunburned back until he went around the corner of the guesthouse and vanished from sight.

"Was what I said so terrible?" Chip asked in surprise. "I don't understand the guy."

"He's touchy," Jack declared. "No two ways about that."

"You know what I think, Jack? I think he's tied in with that burglar. Maybe he *is* the burglar."

"How could he be?" Jack said. "It was right after he passed out that we found Mrs. Wilson tied up."

"I didn't think of that," Chip admitted. "Hey, something just occurred to me. You know, all this might be an act."

"What do you mean, an act?" Jack demanded.

"Have you noticed how we've been meeting up with him? First there was that bit out on the lawn. Then this morning in the dining room. And now he pulls this sore act."

It was Chip's theory that Bob Jillman was trying to draw them into some sort of a confidence game.

"I just feel he's up to something," Chip said. "And

that—that we're the people he's picked to be the suckers."

"What would he be up to?" Jack asked.

"We're going to find out sooner than you think. You'll see." Chip nodded darkly.

"Okay, Chip. You can lay off the melodrama."

It happened shortly after they sat down to lunch. Suddenly Chip leaned close to Jack and whispered, "Take a look. My prediction wasn't just a lot of melodrama."

Jack glanced up. Bob Jillman, wearing a sport shirt and Bermuda shorts, was heading toward their table. He nodded a greeting to the people at the table and sat down opposite the boys.

Jack and Chip didn't have to worry about making conversation. Everyone was discussing the menace of sharks to swimmers. A middle-aged man who looked like a coach or a former professional football player talked with great authority.

"There aren't any sharks around Bermuda," he stated flatly.

A woman paused with her soup spoon halfway to

her mouth. "Well, if I'm bitten by one," she said with mock seriousness, "you'll be hearing from me, Mr. Crossland."

"You're not going to be bitten," Crossland assured her with a hearty self-confidence. "Sharks, you see, follow the inshore edge of the Gulf Stream. So these blessed islands are off their route."

Another woman said she had wanted to go on one of the underwater sightseeing tours to the wrecked ships. She was afraid, however, of encountering—if not a shark—an octopus or another sea monster.

Crossland laughed. He looked directly at Bob and said, "Well, you never know when you might run into a barracuda. They attack swimmers as though it were their favorite pastime." He laughed again. "It isn't without reason they're nicknamed 'tigers of the sea.' "

Bob Jillman spoke then. Everyone turned to look at him, because his voice, in contrast to Crossland's, sounded weak and quavering. "You make diving sound dangerous," Bob said.

"It *is* dangerous," Crossland answered, as though he were as much an authority on diving as on sharks.

"Do you know the greatest danger in diving? Not sharks, or barracuda, or anything else like that that you're liable to meet up with. No sir. It's the diver himself. His fears." Crossland tapped his head significantly. "The fears he's got stored up here."

"I met a shark once," Chip said, innocently buttering a piece of bread.

All eyes turned to him, as they had done when Bob Jillman had spoken.

"You know what I did?" Chip took his time. He put the bread he had buttered into his mouth and chewed it. Everyone waited for him to go on, but he continued to chew. Finally he said, "I just stared at that old shark, who was looking straight at me. Then he swam off."

"They'll run off that way," Crossland stated. "The worst thing you can do—"

"Pardon me," Chip interrupted. "The shark swam off, but he came back." Chip started buttering another piece of bread, moving even more slowly than he had the first time. "He sure did come back."

"Oh, dear," one of the women at the table cried.

Jack kicked at Chip's ankle to get him to stop talking.

"But I fixed him," Chip said mysteriously, "and he didn't come back again."

"What in heaven's name did you do?" the woman who had said "Oh, dear" asked fearfully.

"I had a camera," Chip said, reaching for another slice of bread, "and I hit that shark on the nose with it."

When Jack and Chip left the dining room Chip growled, "What was the big idea of kicking me?"

"Wait till we get outside," Jack answered.

But no sooner were they out on the lawn than Chip said, "I know it was Dad, and not me, who met up with that shark and conked him on the nose. But I was fed up hearing that guy sound off about sharks. I had to get some attention away from him. Let's face it. Wasn't it a lot more dramatic saying I was the one who had tangled with that shark?"

"I shouldn't have kicked you," Jack admitted. "You're right. Somebody had to turn off that wise guy. Crossland is the kind who knows everything. And wasn't that strange? I mean, the way he seemed to be trying to get Bob more on edge than he already is?"

"What did you think of Bob coming to our table?"

Chip asked curiously. "Just the opposite of this morning at breakfast."

Jack scratched his head. "You know what's more interesting?" he said. "The way he reacted to all that shark talk. Did you notice?"

Chip shook his head. "I must have been too busy telling my own shark story."

They came to a group of unoccupied wooden lawn chairs under a tree and sat down.

"I'm telling you, Chip, I could see Bob had turned pale under his sunburn. This is how I figure it. The guy wants to dive, but he's also afraid. He must be scared through and through."

"Golly," Chip said. "If diving's so painful, why doesn't he forget about it?"

"You're overlooking something. He might *have* to dive. He might not be doing it just for fun. I guess he picked up his fins at the desk."

"Look who cometh," Chip muttered under his breath.

Bob Jillman stood outside the door of the house. He looked first to his left, then to his right.

"He'll spot us," Chip said. "Then he'll come this way. Maybe this time he'll tell us what he really wants."

But after looking straight at them Bob went back into the house. In a few minutes he came out, dressed in swimming trunks and carrying a double lung and other diving rig.

"Where does he think he's going?" Jack said, pushing himself up slowly from the chair.

Chip popped to his feet. "We have to stop him. That guy's going to drown himself!"

Jack grabbed Chip. "Let him go!" he ordered sternly.

"Have you flipped?"

Chip tried to shake himself free of Jack's hold. But Jack got a hammerlock on his brother.

"Just hold nice and still," Jack said calmly, keeping a steady pressure on Chip's arm. "And let Bob Jillman go right ahead."

7 *Questions and Answers*

Chip stopped struggling and waited for his brother to let him go. It seemed to him like a very long time. Blaze ran by, exploring an all-absorbing scent.

"Satisfied?" Chip asked finally.

"Remember what you said before, about Bob's putting on an act?" Jack's mouth was close to Chip's ear as he spoke. "Now *this* was an act."

"I bet you're right!" Chip exclaimed. "Let go, will you? You're breaking my arm!"

Jack released his brother. It was evident to them both now that Bob had appeared with an aqualung merely to induce them to follow. They decided that they wouldn't take the bait that easily.

But after returning to the wooden lawn chairs for a while, Chip observed, "Outside of being a little jumpy, Bob's okay. He's a nice enough kind of guy."

"You've changed your mind? Why, before you said—"

"I know—I know what I said, Jack," Chip muttered.

"And now you don't think he's trying to rope us in on some kind of con game?"

Chip once again popped up out of his chair. "Instead of sitting here talking, we'd better get down to the water. If the guy drowns, it'll be our fault."

Chip started off with long strides and Jack followed. After a few moments they reached the spot where they had seen Bob Jillman disappear.

A series of hard-packed earthen steps led down to the guesthouse private beach. At one end of the beach, about thirty feet from where Bob now knelt, a dinghy had been pulled up onto the white sand. Bending low at the waist, the boys scooted for the concealment of the small boat.

"He's going to dive," Chip whispered as he and Jack peeked over the dinghy at Bob. "And if he does, he's going to drown."

Jack was still skeptical. But when Bob began to strap the double-tank aqualung on his back, referring to the instructions in a book that lay opened on the sand, Jack made a decision.

"Come on," he said. He arose and skirted the stern of the dinghy.

Bob didn't even glance up when Jack and Chip approached.

"You know it's us without looking, don't you?" Jack accused, with a resurgence of skepticism. "You expected us. What's the pitch?"

Bob looked up at them from his kneeling position in the sand. "I don't know what you're talking about," he said.

"You can't be serious," Jack said. "You surely don't intend to dive without knowing how."

Bob looked down at the page he'd been reading, as though he were saying, "I'm finding out how."

Suddenly, apparently having come to a decision, he

scrambled to his feet. "All right," he announced, as though to take care of this matter once and for all. "You couldn't understand why I didn't want to go to a regular diving school. I'll tell you why. There's something I have to get off my father's yacht. It sank, but not near all the other wrecks around here. So if it gets out that I'm diving in this out-of-the-way place, everybody'll be sure to think it's for treasure. Divers will swarm all over, and it will be harder than ever to do what I want to do."

Bob's outburst left the boys stunned.

Finally Jack said, "You told us before that you're in a hurry, didn't you?"

"I sure am in a hurry," Bob said. "That's why all those questions you were—"

"And do you remember what we said?" Jack broke in. "Diving's something you can't learn in a hurry."

"I've got it!" Chip exclaimed excitedly. "Jack and I will do the diving for you. You tell us what and where and—"

Bob was shaking his head. "This is something that *I* have to do. Crossland and his talk of sharks bothered me, but—"

"It would be a lot faster if we did it."

"No. You can't. All I can tell you is that it's a personal matter." Bob's voice was firm.

"Okay then, we'll teach you. We'll do it as fast as—as we can." Chip finished the sentence lamely, for he had noticed that Jack hadn't looked too happy about his eagerness to teach Bob.

"Diving lessons aren't cheap, you know," Jack said, obviously trying to cancel Chip's offer.

"That doesn't matter," Bob said.

"Eight dollars an hour. That's what diving schools charge."

"I'll pay you eight," Bob said readily. "That's okay." He paused, looking from Jack to Chip. "What's the matter? Do you want to back out?"

Chip looked at Jack. It was plain he didn't again want to say something of which his older brother would disapprove. He was leaving it up to Jack to answer.

"This isn't the right place to take your first lesson, you know," Jack said to Bob. "The guesthouse pool—that's where we ought to start."

"You mean you'll help me?" Bob said eagerly.

Jack nodded. But he looked thoughtful, as though he were going over the reasons he shouldn't be doing this.

Bob was too pleased and excited to notice. "Can we get started right away? I'll pay you more than eight. I'll pay you ten."

Just before they reached the pool, which was kidney-shaped and on the rear lawn of the house, they stopped. Jack wanted to know how deep Bob would have to be diving. "A hundred-foot dive," he said, "is naturally going to be tougher than—"

"I've got a chart," Bob said. "Would that have the depth indicated on it?"

"Could be," Jack answered.

Bob put his equipment down and went into the house to get the chart.

As soon as their new pupil was out of earshot Chip muttered. "I know. I agreed without thinking. I just felt sorry for the guy. If you want to sock me, go ahead and do it."

"Wait a minute," Jack told Chip. "Don't forget that I approved the whole deal."

"Yeah. Sure. But there wasn't much else you could say."

"I'll admit," Jack said, running the palm of his hand over his red hair, "there are some things that still bother me. Why did Crossland try to scare Bob? Why the hurry? Why is Bob so jumpy? And why couldn't *we* dive and get whatever it is? Come to think of it—he hasn't told us what he's diving for."

"When you get right down to it," Chip added, "Bob hasn't told us much of anything. I'm just glad Dad doesn't know about all this."

"Hey," Jack said suddenly, "what's taking him so long?"

No sooner had Jack spoken than Bob appeared, half running, half walking toward them. He staggered just as he had done before collapsing on the lawn. He stumbled once and just barely managed to regain his balance.

The boys hurried toward him.

Bob was breathing hard and shaking his head in despair. His eyes were brimming with tears. "It's terrible," he muttered, "terrible, terrible. . . ."

8 *The Burning Ocean*

"What's wrong?" Jack asked anxiously.

"Yeah," Chip urged. "What—what gives?"

Bob continued shaking his head in a despairing, hopeless way. "I had it in the trunk," he said. "It's not there, though. And it's not anywhere else."

"Your chart's gone?"

After a thoughtful moment, Jack snapped his fingers and said musingly, "I wonder if—"

"I knew it wasn't any use," Bob went on. "It should have been in the trunk. But, anyhow, I looked all over my room. I pulled out every drawer—didn't know what else to do."

"You think it could be the chart that—" Chip's face brightened.

Jack didn't give Chip a chance to finish. He interrupted, asking Bob if there was an X in red ink on his chart.

Bob's face drained of color. "How did you know that?" he asked incredulously.

"Calm down," Jack said. "We've got your chart. At least I think we have it."

This news delighted Bob, and he bombarded Jack with questions.

"Chip's going to get it," Jack told him. "Let's make sure first that the chart is yours."

Bob's patience soon gave out. He could wait no longer for Chip to come back. He headed for the house, accompanied by Jack. They met Chip as he was coming out the door. Before Chip had a chance to unroll the chart, Bob grabbed the document, looked about surreptitiously, then walked off with it.

As he walked, he unrolled the chart a few inches. He turned to the boys who were following right behind him, a smile lighting up his face.

"That's it, huh?" Chip said.

"Yes. Yes, this is it. But how in the world did you happen to—" Bob looked bewildered.

Jack raised his hands. "It's a long story."

"And weird," Chip added.

Together, they told how a man had come through their bedroom window, left the chart, and hurriedly escaped after stepping on Blaze's tail.

"But why would he leave it in your room?" Bob asked, still perplexed.

"We had just moved into it," Jack said, pursuing a thought that was dawning on him. "Could it be. . . ."

"Could what be?" Chip asked quickly.

"Let's check with Mrs. Wilson and find out who had that room before us," Jack said. "The chart could have been left for him. The character who entered our room might not have known that his friend had departed."

"*I* just moved," Bob said. "I wanted a bigger room and one with an ocean view. They had promised me the first one available."

"Our old room was on the ocean side," Chip offered. "Number five."

"Five!" Bob exclaimed. "Why, that's my room number."

"And you were in eight before?" Jack asked excitedly.

"That's right. Eight."

"Well, we're in eight now. Do you see what this means? The chart was stolen when you were in eight and it was returned to eight. But by that time you had moved out, and we had moved in."

Bob picked up his diving gear. He and the boys strolled toward the pool.

"The guy must have made a copy of the chart," Jack said, "before bringing it back."

"That's for sure," Chip agreed.

"I don't see why he didn't just keep it," Bob mused.

"There might be a reason," Jack said. "The thing is, if the crook could get the chart back to you before you knew it was missing, it would be to his advantage. You wouldn't go to the police and make a big fuss. And it wouldn't put you on your guard, the way you'd be if you knew the chart had been stolen."

"Hey, I just thought of something else," Chip said suddenly.

"What did you think of?" Jack demanded.

"Oh, well. . . ." Chip grinned sheepishly. "What I was thinking—it's kind of confidential. I better not say anything."

They stopped at the pool and looked down at the placid, pale green water. They were the only people near the pool area.

After a moment Jack asked, "Do you have any idea, Bob, who might have taken it—and brought it back?"

Bob didn't answer right away.

"How about that X on the chart?" Chip asked. "The first thing we thought of was treasure when we noticed it. So maybe that's what the crook was thinking, too."

"But I haven't the least idea who he would be," Bob declared.

They looked silently down at the water for some time, waiting for an idea to occur to them. Jack checked the chart and saw that the depth at the X was forty-five feet.

"Not too deep," Chip said, relief plain in his voice.

But Bob said, "This is getting kind of—oh, I don't know, maybe dangerous. We know this crook isn't going to stop now. So, uh—uh—if you fellows want to back out. . . ." He shrugged his thin, sunburned shoulders. "It's okay—if you want to." Burdened with the twin aqualung, and with an unhappy expression on his face, Bob made a pathetic figure.

"Aw, no," Jack said, smiling in an attempt to put Bob at ease. "Not if you still intend to pay us eight dollars an hour. You can put your rig down. You won't need any of it for your first few lessons."

To begin, Bob had to swim the width of the pool underwater. Next he swam on the surface with a weight belt weighing six pounds.

"That's just to make it more interesting," Chip said, grinning.

"I'll tell you what it's really for," Jack offered, looking down at Bob who was breathing hard and clinging tightly to the edge of the pool. "When you come up after a dive you're going to have to be able to swim with your equipment, since the boat's not always going to be right where you hoped it would be. Get out now, will you, Bob? I've some stuff to tell you."

"What's the matter?" Bob asked worriedly as soon

as he had climbed out of the deep end of the pool.

"You're doing great," Chip said.

"Relax," Jack told Bob. "Relaxing is more important than anything. Now before I start my spiel, I've got a question. How are you? In good shape? If you're not, you know, you ought not to dive. I'm not talking about tip-top condition. I mean, is your heart okay? That kind of thing."

Bob hesitated. "Sure, I'm all right. But I've got to dive, no matter what."

"Okay," Jack said. "But at least we ought to tell you the risks involved in diving."

"I just remembered something," Chip said. "What happened to you the other night? You passed out, didn't you?"

Bob squirmed. "Yes," he admitted reluctantly. The boys waited for him to go on. "I had one of those twenty-four-hour viruses. Instead of waiting to get over it, I went out with a snorkel to get accustomed to the water. That, plus all the sun, really affected me."

Jack and Chip nodded.

"The next morning I was fine. It was just one of

those twenty-four-hour bugs."

"Okay," Jack said. "Now I'm going to tell you what we were told when we started diving. That fellow at lunch—Mr. Crossland, who knew all about sharks—was right about one thing. I mean, when he said the big danger was all the fears you had up here." Jack tapped his head the way Crossland had done. "You have to control them or you're a goner. You know that if you're trapped in a burning building, panic, and jump out a window, you're a dead duck. The ocean isn't burning, but it will get you just the way a fire will, if you don't keep your head."

Bob fidgeted with impatience. He was clearly anxious to begin learning more important things.

"How about showing him how to clear his faceplate?" Chip suggested. "A faceplate is a mask," he explained.

"Yeah," Jack said. "We'll get to that now. All right," he directed Bob, "go ahead and put it on."

As Bob put on the faceplate, Jack explained that the air space between one's face and the glass made it possible to see underwater. Water creeping under the glass might frighten him, Jack continued, because it cut down on visibility and gave the impression that he was going to breathe the water and drown.

Just then Blaze came at a lope toward the pool. At sight of Bob wearing the faceplate, the dog began to bark furiously. Chip went off to tie up the dog.

"I'll be right back," Jack told Bob hurriedly, who by this time had removed the faceplate. "Chip might need some help with the hound."

Chip didn't need any help. All Jack wanted was an excuse to talk to his brother.

"When I asked him what kind of shape he was in," Jack said, "I couldn't bring myself to say, 'How's your nerve? Do you get rattled easily?' "

"Why would you want to ask him that?" Chip said, rubbing Blaze's head. "Look at him, just look at him, and you've got your answer."

Jack shook his head worriedly. "Diving with him is going to be terribly dangerous."

"Dangerous?" Chip repeated despairingly. "It will be suicide! Why, diving alone is a lot safer than diving with someone like Bob!"

9 *A Shaky Beginning*

"We'd better get back," Jack said. "Bob's probably flipped by now. But what are we going to do?"

Chip stopped rubbing Blaze's head. "We've got to dive with the guy. What else?"

They walked off a few steps and stopped. Blaze watched them intently.

"Everyone gets discouraged at first, diving," Jack said. "Someone like Bob is sure to." Chip nodded.

"And that's when we might get him to change his mind," Jack continued. "Really bear down, then convince him he ought to let us do the diving for him."

Chip shrugged. "Well, let's see what happens."

Chip started off, but Jack stopped him. "What was that confidential thing you said you didn't want to talk about."

"Oh," Chip said, remembering. "You know what I thought? That maybe the guy who broke into Mrs. Wilson's safe—"

Jack nodded. "The same thing occurred to me," he said.

"You mean that the guy thought Bob's chart would be there?"

"Right," Jack said. "In a place like this, people usually leave their valuables in the office safe."

As soon as they had returned to the pool, Jack went into the water at the shallow end. He was wearing the faceplate. Both Chip and Bob stood in the water with him.

"The first thing you have to learn, Bob," Jack said, "is how to clear your faceplate. It will take a little practice, but it's not difficult. Just—just watch me."

Jack sank down in the pool and put on the faceplate while underwater. When he rose out of the water, there was no water inside the mask.

Jack took off the faceplate and handed it to Bob. "Now, I want you to do what I did. You get the water out with air pressure. This is how. You press the right side of the faceplate with your hand—your right hand —then turn your head to the left and blow hard through your nose." Jack repeated. "Understand?"

Bob went through the steps while standing in shallow water.

"It'll be a lot different down in the water," Chip warned Bob.

"Remember always keep your eyes open," Jack said as a last-minute piece of advice.

The boys watched as Bob went down with the faceplate. The pale green water was perfectly clear. They saw Bob put the faceplate on and begin to follow the instructions Jack had given.

Suddenly Bob started to thrash wildly underwater. In a second he shot up, clawing at the faceplate with both hands. As soon as he surfaced, he freed himself of the faceplate, gasping desperately for air.

Chip started to talk, but Jack shook his head from side to side, signaling him to remain silent. "Give him a chance to recover," he muttered.

At last Bob had caught his breath and could speak. "It was awful," he told them. "That water clamped tight to my face. It made me feel as if I were drowning."

"Did you keep your eyes open, the way I said?" Jack asked, a little sharply.

"All I wanted," Bob answered, "was to get that faceplate off. And fast. That must be the way you feel when you're drowning. All that water was up my nose. . . ." He shook his head, as though trying to rid himself of the memory.

"I'm sorry, Bob," Jack said more kindly. "But clearing your faceplate is one thing you've got to do if you're going to dive."

"Once you get the hang of it—"

"But I didn't even try," Bob broke in on Chip despairingly. "I didn't even begin to do any of the things you and Jack said."

"That's okay," Jack told him, in an attempt to belittle what had happened. "It's all part of learning."

Bob let out a long, weary sigh. He shook his head at what a fool he'd been and moved a few steps away

from the boys, down the side of the pool.

"Well, he got discouraged fast," Chip whispered to Jack. "Maybe now we can talk him into letting us do the diving."

"Shhh," Jack said, for Bob had turned and was moving toward them. Then he called out to Bob, "I might as well tell you that if you're going to dive you've got to learn to control yourself."

"Yes," Bob said, nodding. He sighed again. "I know."

"You want to change your mind?" Chip asked. "I mean about our doing the diving instead of you."

Bob shook his head. "I can't," he said. "You don't understand."

"Chip's not the only one," Jack said.

Bob was thoughtful for a moment. "I have to dive!" he declared firmly. After hesitating again, he added, "I told you that I personally have to get something off the *Texas Queen,* my father's yacht."

"You have to get something?" Jack asked curiously.

"Right," Bob said.

It was plain to the boys that Bob didn't want to tell

them what it was that he had to recover from the sunken yacht.

"Guess there's only one thing to do," Jack said. "Get to work."

Bob's instruction continued in the pool. Before too long, he was able to put on both the lung and the faceplate underwater. He was taught how, in an emergency, two divers could breathe from a single lung by passing the mouthpiece back and forth between them. He jumped backward into the pool wearing his twin lung and holding his faceplate with both hands to keep it from coming off. This was the way he would have to leave the boat when diving began in earnest in the ocean.

As days passed, Bob's confidence increased. His sunburn turned a deep tan. When they finished the training that could be learned in a pool, he asked in a small voice, "It's going to be a lot different diving in the ocean, isn't it?"

"Different?" Jack said, appearing reluctant to answer.

"Okay." Bob held up his hands. "I get the message. It's going to be a lot different."

"Naturally, going down deep is something you've got to adjust to," Chip ventured.

"And according to the chart," Bob said, "the *Texas Queen* is forty-five feet down."

"The main thing is never to panic," Jack said firmly, "no matter what."

And Chip advised, "Play it cool. That's all you've got to do."

Bob was looking oddly at Jack and didn't even seem to hear Chip. "When you said, 'No matter what,' just what did you mean?" he asked cautiously.

"What do you want me to do, scare you?"

"I'd like to know what to expect. Is that going to scare me?"

"Well, I can tell you what you're going to start thinking when you go down deeper and deeper—"

"And deeper," Chip put in.

"You'll think what everybody thinks," Jack continued. "But you'll feel that you're the only one who ever thought anything like that. And you'll wonder if you're a coward."

"I'll wish I was back on the boat, huh?" Bob said.

"I'm not saying that thought won't cross your mind," Jack answered. "But there's another thing that you'll probably think. 'If anything goes wrong,' you'll think, 'I've got an awfully long way to get to the top. I'll never make it in time.' "

"And you might as well tell him, Jack," Chip suggested, "how easy it is to get lost—or to think you're lost."

"The main thing—"

"I know," Bob broke in on Jack, "the main thing is not to panic. Because if I do— well, it's not only the end of me, but I might be risking your neck and Chip's."

Chip didn't say anything.

Jack said, "I guess you've got enough of a briefing. Tomorrow we'll do a little ocean diving. What do you say?"

They began to move away from the pool.

"I don't want you pampering me," Bob said determinedly. "I feel you've been doing that all along. And I'm in a hurry. I want to start right off and dive for the *Texas Queen*. Yeah. *Yeah*. Tomorrow!"

"I wish you luck," a voice behind them said.

The boys whirled around, startled. It was Crossland, the self-proclaimed expert on all things beneath the surface of the sea. There was something mysterious and sinister about his sudden appearance. And his smirking smile canceled the luck he had just wished Bob.

10 *Self-Doubts and Time-Outs*

When Jack, dressed in pajamas, opened the Venetian blinds the next day, brilliant sunlight flooded the room. What he had done, he saw, had had no effect in waking Chip. He started to open the blind of the other window, then decided to take more positive action.

But before he could go across the room to shake his brother, Chip sat up slowly in bed. He shielded his eyes from the sun and grumbled about the noise Jack was making.

"Today's the day, you know," Jack said.

"Will you fix that thing so that the sun—" Chip stopped abruptly. Suddenly things began to register.

"Oh, yeah," he said, wincing as though in great pain. He fell back onto the bed and groaned, "Why did you wake me?"

"You don't have to dive," Jack said, taking off his pajama top. "Stay in the boat. I'll go down with him."

"That would be worse. I'd be wondering all the time what was going on. Especially after the strange way in which Crossland wished Bob luck."

"You want to take those pictures for Dad, don't you?"

Chip sat up in bed again, saying, "What's bothering me now is that Bob's getting confident. And yet he hasn't really stopped being jittery—that's the thing."

Jack continued dressing. He came out of the bathroom when he was in the middle of brushing his teeth. In spite of a mouthful of lather, he mumbled, "We're liable to meet up with this guy who stole the chart. I mean, meet up with him down in the water—when we dive."

Chip was out of bed now and dressing. "Maybe he's already got what Bob's after. So Bob's going to be like the anchor man in a relay race when the other side has already run their last man and won."

"Wonder when he's going to tell us what he's after," Jack said. "Or *if* he's going to."

Just then there was a knock at the door, so timid it could hardly be heard. Chip answered, walking in an up-and-down way because he had on only one shoe.

Both Jack and Chip were surprised to see Bob standing in the doorway. By the solemn, embarrassed expression on his face, it appeared that he'd overheard their conversation. But there was no way of knowing just how much he had heard.

"Well, today's the day," Jack said brightly. He wanted to break the tension in the room.

Bob merely nodded.

The silence came back, heavier than before.

Jack stammered, "We were just talking about—"

"Pardon me," Bob said, taking a wallet from the hip pocket of his shorts. "I want to pay you for the time you spent teaching me."

"No." Jack shook his head. "Oh, no. Wait till we do all the diving."

"We have," Bob said, "as far I'm concerned."

"What's wrong?" Chip asked. "If it's because you overheard us say—"

"He's discouraged, can't you see?" Jack muttered to Chip. "But what I want to know is why."

"It's not that I'm discouraged," Bob said, as if answering Jack. He moved to the bed and sat down, keeping his eyes on the floor. "I wish that's all it was."

After a moment's pause he admitted that he was afraid to dive in the ocean. He looked so unhappy that the boys forgot all about their having wanted him to become discouraged and give up.

"That's a good sign," Jack said cheerily, in an attempt to snap the boy out of his depression.

"Sure is," Chip agreed.

"I was that way before I made my first dive. So was Chip."

"And how!" Chip nodded emphatically.

Bob looked up at the boys, obviously trying to decide if they meant what they were saying.

"If you want to know how I feel about your diving," Jack said, "I'll tell you. You decided to start off by diving to the *Texas Queen*."

"That's what I said," Bob admitted, "but—"

"Well, that's what we ought to do. I was doubtful at first, but now I—"

Bob stood up. "That doesn't make sense, does it? You mean I'm ready now, because I'm scared?"

Jack nodded. "Right. That means you're keyed up and—and alert."

Chip tried to smile encouragingly, but the smile was beginning to crack. "Do you know what you're doing?" he wanted to demand of Jack. "We shouldn't dive with this guy at all if he's scared."

In the harbor in Hamilton the boys rented *For Keeps,* a sixteen-foot outboard. It was a daily rental which included Samson the skipper. Samson, they were to discover, always wore a grease-smudged T-shirt, a blue yachting cap with an embossed crown that hung onto the cap by only a few threads. He never had anything to say, and he was always unshaven.

When Bob showed Samson the chart the skipper barely glanced at it before starting the motor and heading out of the harbor. He sat up high, on top of the seat's back, with his feet on the seat. He had to lean forward to keep his hand on the wheel. But his visibility was improved. From this position he could see over the windshield.

The boat pitched. Each time it came down, it hit the water with a hard thud, making the trip extremely uncomfortable.

When even Samson seemed to have had enough of the rough ride, he eased the throttle back to neutral. Then he made a gesture with his hand, a gesture which could have meant anything. Jack took it to mean that Samson wanted another look at the chart. And he was right, for the skipper took the chart when it was handed to him. After another glance at the X on the chart, he went into action. He turned off the motor, threw the anchor overboard, and pressed a button on the dash which caused the motor to tilt forward and the propeller to rise out of the water. Then he manually raised the canopy, which shaded all but the stern of the boat. Without a word, he lay down. He lay on his side, cushioning his head with both hands.

The boys and Bob began to put on their gear.

Chip went over first, Bob next, and Jack last. At once they proceeded downward, holding onto the anchor line.

Bob was at nine feet, according to the depth gauge on Jack's arm, when there was the first sign of trouble. Bob stopped and pointed to his ears, an indication that they were hurting him. Jack motioned for him to continue downward.

Bob shook his head and started climbing back up the rope. But when he reached the fins on Jack's feet he went into reverse and headed down the rope again.

Except for the singing of the lung regulators, all was silence. The movements of the three were the effortless movements of the images in dreams. The world had become a green fluid one. The bubbles streaming upward from the lungs somehow added to the sense of unreality. A school of silver bream went by. Bob and the boys stopped once to clear their ears of water, something Bob should have done earlier when he complained about his ears hurting, Jack realized too late.

Finally, as through a haze, the bottom of the ocean could be seen. For a while the boys swam above the sandy bottom with its sparse grass and various types of coral, all the time keeping within sight of the anchor line. Soon they realized that, the *Texas Queen* was nowhere near them.

They swam farther afield, still searching. Suddenly Jack and Chip realized that Bob wasn't with them. They had seen him one minute, but he was gone the next.

The boys swam back and forth frantically, keeping in sight of one another. Soon they came to a small hill of coral. Beyond it they saw a vast plain of sand and not a sign of Bob.

They searched as much as they could, always within easy reach of the anchor line. Finally Jack pointed to his watch and then pointed up, indicating that they had better head up the anchor line.

Chip shook his head. He didn't want to leave, knowing Bob was wandering around hopelessly lost.

Jack kept pointing to his watch. They had to leave, he gestured. Soon their supply of air would be exhausted. They couldn't possibly take any more time to look for Bob. If they did it would mean death for all of them.

11 *Tracking a Clue*

Jack and Chip went up the anchor line. Jack led the way, setting the pace. The need for speed was urgent, but they took their time. They both knew that if they ascended too fast an air embolism would result, causing injured lungs.

Chip was right at Jack's heels when he climbed up the ladder and into the boat. The boys looked around eagerly, ignoring Samson, who now sat with his feet up, drinking a bottle of bright orange soda. They were both hoping desperately that somehow Bob had arrived ahead of them.

It took only a glance to see that Bob wasn't on board.

Jack looked at his watch. "By now he has to be on his reserve air supply." He twisted about worriedly. "We showed him how to turn it on. I hope—"

"We did more than show him," Chip said. "We drilled him—a lot."

"Yeah, but in a clutch would he remember? That's the thing. You know Bob—the type he is."

After downing the last of the soda, Samson said lazily, "Trouble?"

Jack glanced at his watch. "Even his reserve air supply must be about gone."

"We don't know what happened to Bob," Chip said to Samson slowly. "He—he just disappeared."

Samson grunted, the only indication he had even heard.

Jack rushed to where the spare tanks of air were lined up on deck. Chip didn't have to ask him if he was going down again. Instead of wasting time talking, Chip got busy exchanging his empty tanks for full ones.

Suddenly the boys heard Samson's yell from the bow of the boat. When the boys rushed forward Samson

was headed for the anchor line.

"It's Bob!" Chip yelled excitedly. "Do you see him? Right there!"

Jack didn't take time to answer. He ran to help Samson get the anchor up. Chip moved quickly along the catwalk to the prow of the boat and shouted to Bob. Though distant, Bob's splashing was plainly visible. "Don't swim, Bob. We'll get you. Just float, float!" Chip yelled hoarsely.

When the *For Keeps* pulled alongside of Bob, he grabbed the ladder and started coming aboard.

Jack was so glad to see him that he laughed nervously. "Boy, you're getting real service!" he said.

"Where did you go, Bob?" Chip asked, smiling in relief. "For a walk?"

Samson watched the scene wordlessly.

"Am I glad to be here!" Bob gasped, as soon as his faceplate was off. "I was never so glad to be anyplace in my life."

"You must have used your air reserve," Jack said.

Bob nodded. "I looked for you as long as I could. I figured it down to the last second."

"We worried you might forget how to use the reserve," Chip said.

"Was I scared!" Bob said. "I don't know what happened. It just seemed like I turned around and you were gone. Then everything down there looked the same. I—I didn't know where I was."

"I don't want anything like *that* happening again," Jack declared firmly.

"What about the *Texas Queen?*" Bob asked suddenly. "I wandered around a lot. And if she was around I'd have seen her."

Chip whispered so that Samson wouldn't hear. "You think he took us to the right spot?" he asked.

Jack shrugged. Bob said Samson seemed to know what he was doing.

"Wrecks get covered by sand and stuff," Jack said thoughtfully. "But that takes time."

"Why, it hasn't been two years since Dad's boat went down," Bob reminded Jack.

Samson, who had been forward, came toward them with a freshly opened bottle of orange soda.

"You sure we dived at the right spot?" Jack asked.

Samson nodded. That and a grunt expressed complete authority.

The three boys sat in the stern on the way back to Hamilton. A yellow-green ribbon of water ran through the middle of the effervescent V-shaped wake. They watched the wake until the fumes from the motor became too strong for them.

As they looked at Samson, once again perched high above the wheel, Jack said, "I just thought of something. That X might have been changed by the crook before he returned the chart."

"Hey!" Chip exclaimed. "Maybe it was!"

"When you first looked at the chart," Jack said to Bob, "do you remember if the X was in a different place?"

"I didn't look at it that closely," Bob said. "Anyhow, how would I remember something like that?"

"It might have been changed then," Jack said. "That would give the crook a chance to search the wreck, without your barging in on him."

"Where could we check?" Bob asked, excited by this new possibility. "The police, do you think? Do they keep a record of all the wrecks?"

"I doubt that they would," Jack said.

Chip pointed to Samson, saying, "I guess there's no point in asking him. He'd have to talk to tell us. And you know how hard it is for him to talk."

After going down Front Street near the harbor, the boys turned off on Queen Street and came to the library.

"How about stopping in here?" Jack said.

"You mean to find out where the police station is?" Chip asked.

"The more I think about it," Jack mused, "the more leery I am about going to the police. First of all, they probably wouldn't have the dope we want. And they might come out to see us at the guesthouse, which would be sure to panic Mrs. Wilson."

The librarian was tall, thin, and elegant-looking. She shook her head when they asked her if she had a record of the wrecks around Bermuda. By the expression on her face, she seemed to be in pain because she couldn't provide the information for which they had asked.

Suddenly she brightened, as though struck by inspiration. She murmured a few sentences, but her heavy

British accent made understanding her impossible.

The boys and Bob thanked her.

She seemed to appreciate their thanks so much that Chip added, "You've been a lot of help. You sure have."

Outside Bob said, "Maybe we should have asked her to write it down. She wouldn't have written with that accent."

"She'd probably turn out," Chip said, "to have one of those handwritings you can't read. And if you had to ask her what she'd written, you'd be right back where you started."

They wandered aimlessly down the street. At the corner a white-gloved traffic policeman directed traffic. Because he stood so straight and his arm gestures were so stiff and carefully executed, it looked as if he were doing something much more important than directing traffic. A fringed surrey went by, with the clop-clop of the horse's hooves. Then a few noisy, motorized bikes.

"Maybe we'll be able to understand that cop," Bob said. "Shall we ask him?"

But when they started to cut across the street to the spot where he stood, the policeman stopped them by holding up his white-gloved hand. While they waited, Jack spotted a sign down the street that read THE MID-ATLANTIC NEWS.

"Why didn't we think of that before?" Chip exclaimed as the three of them walked hurriedly toward the newspaper office. "Do you know the date of the wreck, Bob?"

"As well as I know my birthday. It'll be two years ago that it happened. On this coming October fourteenth."

They had no trouble understanding the tall, bald-headed man in the newspaper office. He was very cooperative, too.

While they were going through the paper dated October fourteenth they realized that the wreck wouldn't have been reported until the next day.

They quickly got the paper for the fifteenth. They went all the way through it, without finding any mention of the wreck.

Jack looked up at the top of one of the pages. "It's October fifteenth. We have the right paper all right."

They went through the paper again, this time more

slowly and much more carefully.

"That's funny," Jack said. "A wreck like that. They'd surely have something about it in the paper, wouldn't they?"

Bob said, "You'd think so."

While Jack and Bob had been talking, Chip had been idly leafing through the paper for the third time. "Say, look at this!" he exclaimed, pointing to the top of one of the pages. "Page ten. And the next number, you see, is thirteen."

"A whole page has been torn out!" Bob exclaimed.

"And I'll bet that's the page," Jack said firmly, "that's got the dope we're looking for."

12 *A Test of Courage*

"I know who tore the page out," Chip cried excitedly. "It must have been the guy who changed the chart."

"Could be," Jack admitted. "We can't be sure, though."

"How do we even know," Bob said, "that the missing page had anything about the wreck on it?"

"Anything wrong?" a voice asked.

The boys and Bob had been huddled over the paper. They looked up and saw that it was the tall, bald newspaperman who had spoken.

"Somebody tore a page out," Chip said, pointing to the paper.

"And it could be just the one we're looking for," Jack added quickly.

The tall man folded his arms and looked thoughtful for a few moments. Then he spoke to them. "I was just thinking," he said, "of someone else who called for the paper of that particular date. It was a very short time ago. No. He wasn't at all the type who would go in for vandalism."

Chip jumped up. "What did he look like?"

"A big man. A certain dignity about him. Not the sort—as I said—who'd stoop to tearing—"

"Pardon me," Jack said, and he stood up, too. "Do you have another copy of this paper—the same date?"

"No," the man said. A smile came to his face along with the distant, thoughtful expression. "Curious," he said. "This person we've been talking about asked the very same thing. I'll tell you why I remember. I distinctly recall that I told him about our plans to get all these old papers on microfilm."

"Hey, fellows," Jack said, "this all makes sense now. After changing the chart he'd naturally want to get rid of any other record of where—"

Jack broke off abruptly, as the newspaperman was listening with great interest to what he was saying.

"It's just my opinion," the newspaperman said, "but I still don't think this individual would go in for any high jinks. A cultured, well-informed man. You said a chart of yours was changed? Was it altered with criminal intent?"

Jack shook his head to stop Chip from answering.

Bob said hurriedly, "We'd better go."

"Oh, I see," the newspaperman said. "You don't want to say anything for fear it'll get in the paper. But I'm not a reporter. Oh, no, I just work here in the office. Now you listen to me." He smiled kindly. "If you don't tell me what this is all about, after arousing my interest the way you have, I'll consider it a dirty trick."

"You're not just saying all this?" Chip asked doubtfully. "I know reporters use all kinds of gimmicks to get stories."

"That they do," the man agreed. "But I told you I'm not a reporter. I can't even write a note to the milkman that he understands."

A pudgy man in a white, rumpled suit suddenly

appeared. He shook the tall man's hand and slapped him on the shoulder. "You've made my day, Ken," he said. "Your admission that you can't write is most refreshing. Every reporter on this paper thinks he can write and—sad to say—he can't."

Ken introduced the man to the boys. He praised him highly as a reporter.

"And Reynolds' memory is phenomenal," Ken continued. "I'll wager he can tell you what you were looking for in that paper. The paper is only a couple of years old. Ask him—and you'll see."

"The *Texas Queen* was wrecked—" Bob began.

"You must be Jillman's son," Reynolds broke in. "I see the resemblance."

"Did you know my father?" Bob asked, completely flabbergasted.

"He complimented me. That's a boost to anybody's memory. He said I'd go places because I'm an enterprising reporter. That was just a little while before he died. Of course, he was wrong about the enterprising bit. It's quite apparent I'm still here on the *Mid-Atlantic News*. He raised onions, didn't he? Bermuda onions in

Texas. Very wealthy. I did a story on how he rose in the world on sheer courage and determination. Too bad about his boat. I remember when it was wrecked."

"I told you," Ken said proudly, "he remembers everything. Ask him—go ahead and ask what you want to know."

Jack put the question to Reynolds. Without saying a word the pudgy reporter took a piece of scratch paper off a desk and started drawing. He put down the exact location of the wrecked *Texas Queen*—on the coral reef on the north shore, instead of south of Warwick Long Bay, where the X on the chart had pinpointed it. It was evidently nearer the other wrecks.

"I can sense you don't want this story published yet," Reynolds said. "Okay, okay, just give it to me a few minutes before it breaks—if it breaks. That's all I ask."

Outside the newspaper office the boys paused for a moment. They were uncertain as to what to do next.

Bob folded the paper Reynolds had given him and put it in his pocket.

"Whoever tore out that page," Chip said, "ought to have done something about Reynolds. I mean, because he's able to pass along the same information. You wouldn't think he's such a hot reporter, would you? The way he's dressed and all."

"Bob," Jack said, pursuing his own thoughts, "we're not going to be able to have so much privacy for our diving now."

"I know," Bob said. "We'll have to dive around all the other wrecks."

"But at the western tip. At least that's a break."

"Hey, you know what time it is?" Chip said suddenly. "No wonder I'm hungry. It's a quarter of three."

They picked a restaurant near the harbor. Fish tanks which were all lit up served as decorations. Chip complained of the slow service because he was hungry. The delay appeared to bother Bob even more. "I've only got three weeks," he said.

Chip laughed. "Golly, we ought to be waited on by then."

Bob apparently didn't think that was funny. After a moment of serious thought he said, "Maybe it would be best if I let you in on what this is all about."

And he proceeded to do so. Without interruption he

told them that he had to recover a figurine from the *Texas Queen* by September seventh, a date only three weeks away. The figurine was the original model for the "giant" used on the label of "Jillman's Jiant Bermuda Onions." If he didn't recover the figurine from the yacht by September seventh, he wouldn't inherit the bulk of his father's estate.

Chip wanted to know why Bob's father had made such an unusual will.

"It's just as Reynolds said," Bob told Chip. "Dad was a self-made man. He got where he did on his own—by hard work and a lot of courage. I know Dad didn't mean to make it tough for me. It sure was hard though, trying to live up to the standard he'd set. I was a disappointment to him. I know I was. His will didn't surprise me at all. He just wanted me to prove I was worthy of being an heir of his."

"But why would a crook want this figurine?" Jack asked. "It must be valuable. Is it?"

Bob shook his head. "Not that valuable. But if I don't recover it my inheritance will go to somebody else. So it is valuable—in a way. To me, it's a challenge and—and very, very important. It'll mean that I haven't let Dad down and—"

"You can do a lot in three weeks," Jack said encouragingly. "You're already a diver. You proved that this morning."

"Did I?" Bob asked. "Can you say that, after what happened?"

Chip twisted about in his seat, startled.

"What's the matter?" Jack asked.

Chip turned back. "For a second there," he explained, "I was sure I spotted Reynolds. It's kind of hard to believe, you know, that a reporter wouldn't be on the trail of a story if he thought there was one."

Their food finally came.

While they were eating, Bob asked if they could make another dive that day.

"I was right, wasn't I," Jack told Bob, "when I said you'd become a diver? It's in your blood, once you make a deep dive like that."

"You're wrong, Jack," Bob said. "I'm just as scared now as I ever was."

He looked thoughtful for a moment. Suddenly a

greenish pallor seeped through his tan. It was clear he hadn't turned pale because of what he'd said. What frightened him was whatever he was staring at.

"What's the matter?" both Chip and Jack chorused.

Bob continued to stare. "Don't turn around," he whispered. And as much as the boys wanted to turn and discover the cause of their friend's fear, they remained rigid in their seats.

13 *Trouble Arrives*

"Who is it?" Chip asked. "Come on, tell us. Is it that reporter?"

Bob fidgeted. It was plain he hadn't even heard Chip. He put his napkin on the table, as though he were through eating and getting ready to leave.

"Can't you tell us who it is?" Jack persisted. "Make it seem like part of our conversation."

Bob didn't appear to have listened to Jack, either. Suddenly he rose and headed for the door.

Jack and Chip jumped up and hurried after him. When they heard a shout behind them, they both turned quickly, expecting to see the person from whom Bob was running. But it was the waiter who was rushing after them with their check held high in the air.

Without slowing down, Jack reached back and took the check from the waiter.

"Go!" Jack urged Chip as they reached the cashier. "Catch Bob! Hold onto him while I take care of this!"

But Bob returned just then. He had his wallet out and was hurriedly taking bills from it. Quite obviously it hadn't been until he was outside that he had realized he'd forgotten to pay for his lunch.

Bob continued to hurry, and so the boys didn't have a chance to question him on the way out of the building. Then they had to run, for Bob had spotted a cab across the street and was sprinting for it.

They all took a little time to catch their breath after the cab started off.

"It couldn't have been that reporter," Jack said, "who made you leave the way you did."

"We didn't have any dessert, you know," Chip grumbled.

"Why else would he be here?" Bob muttered to himself. "It can only be for one reason. . . ."

Chip looked at Jack in disgust. "What gives, Bob?" he demanded. "Let us in on this big mystery, for crying out loud!"

Before Bob could answer, Jack said to him, "You saw someone whom you suspect—of something. But this person must be kind of close to you. That's why you still have to convince yourself—"

"You're right," Bob said, surprised.

"I still don't get it," Chip said.

"He's my cousin," Bob said, "but—"

"Your cousin?" Chip said incredulously. "You mean just a cousin could get you so hot and bothered?"

"Lenny's here to stop me from bringing up that figurine," Bob explained. "I'm sure of it."

"If he does, will he get your share of the will?" Jack asked.

"His mother would get my share. But Aunt Evelyn's great. She wouldn't even think of doing anything crooked."

"But Lenny's different?" Jack asked.

"I'm not saying he's crooked. But he's—well, I guess aggressive is the word. And why would he be here in

Bermuda, at just this time, if it wasn't to—"

"I know you just saw him for the first time," Jack said. "I'm wondering, though, how long he's been here."

"You mean he might be the one who stole the chart?" Chip asked.

"Yes." Jack nodded. "And returned it after changing the position of the X on it."

"That trick almost worked, too," Bob said. "I—I was just lucky this morning, figuring the reserve air supply just right."

"Bob," Jack said, "this cousin of yours, does he fit the description that newspaperman gave us? You remember, of the guy he didn't think would tear a page out of the paper."

Bob shook his head. "No," he said. "Lenny's not dignified. How else did he describe him?"

"Cultured," Jack said. "I think that was the word he used."

Bob shook his head again. "That's not Lenny," he said. "But he might have hired someone who is like that."

The cab pulled into the driveway of the guesthouse and the boys got out. As soon as they had left the cab Chip asked Bob, "Why did you run like that? Would it have hurt you to talk to your cousin?"

"Right now," Bob admitted, "the way I acted seems real nutty. What happened was that I panicked."

"That's for sure," Chip said.

"Well, I do know I had the feeling Lenny was out to keep me from getting that figurine."

"Or this might be delayed panic from this morning," Jack said. "You were lost—forty-five feet down—and didn't panic then."

They continued to stand outside the guesthouse. Their conversation turned to what they should do next.

"Whether Lenny's mixed up in this or not," Bob said, "I still have to dive."

"Oh, sure," Chip said.

"I mean dive today. Right now. I don't know what trick Lenny or somebody else is liable to pull. I've got to get that figurine. . . . Look, there's another cab pulling in. I've got my nerve back now—I'm going right down to the harbor."

He hurried away from the boys in his readiness to enter the approaching cab.

"We can't dive now," Chip told his brother anxiously. "Does he think you can make deep dives two times in a row, just like that?"

Jack nodded thoughtfully. "Probably. How would he know any different?"

They moved toward Bob. But before they could speak to him, the cab pulled up and the rear door opened.

"Hey, Bob," the person who was getting out of the cab exclaimed, "I was wondering when I was going to run into you!"

Bob's hand was still being shaken as the cab turned and went off down the drive. Chip glanced at Jack and shrugged as though to say, "I certainly don't know what this is all about."

"Are these friends of yours, Bob?" the young fellow who had come out of the cab was saying. "Why don't you introduce me? Don't bother. I'll take care of it. I'm Lenny Thomas, Bob's cousin."

Lenny shook the boys' hands as he went on talking.

He had an overpowering personality. The sparkle of his eyes suggested confidence and conceit rather than good nature. And although he wasn't any older than Bob, his manner and rugged physique made him appear so.

"I'm registered here," Lenny was saying to Bob. "It's not a coincidence. Mother told me where to find you. We'll have a ball for ourselves. And since you've been here a while and know the ropes, you can show me around."

"I've got a job to do," Bob said. His words sounded more like a plea than a protest.

"Oh, I know all about that," Lenny said vaguely. "Come on inside and we'll talk." He excused himself and went off with his unwilling cousin in tow.

"Golly!" Chip exclaimed. "Now I know why Bob ran when he saw that guy."

"Lenny's the one who should be diving. He'd have that figurine in no time." Jack was overwhelmed.

"Hey," Chip said, "maybe he's got it. He could have been diving for it. If he was the one who swiped the chart, he'd know just where to dive."

Jack shook his head. "If he had the figurine, there would be no reason for him to remain in Bermuda. And why would he be making up to Bob the way he's doing? No, he hasn't got that figurine. But he's going to get it. Or else he's going to keep Bob from getting it."

"Come on," Chip said. "Let's save Bob from that guy."

"I think we're too late," Jack answered numbly. "Look!"

14 *Unwelcome Visitor*

Chip looked just in time to see Lenny push Bob into the cab, jump in himself, then slam the cab's door after him.

Oddly, after making the turn in front of the guest-house, the cab came speeding back. Chip ran out in the drive and waved his arms in an attempt to flag it down. The cab squealed to a stop a distance beyond him, and both boys started running toward the cab. It immediately started up again, leaving the boys standing in the middle of the drive.

"Of course it was Lenny," Jack declared, "who told the cabbie to keep going."

"What's he going to do to Bob?" Chip asked anxiously.

"You saw how Lenny shoved him into the cab. It didn't look very good, did it?"

"Is he kidnapping him, do you think?"

Jack scowled. "Hardly," he said. "But I'll bet he's up to something." He scratched his head, a worried, puzzled expression on his face. "That's the cab Lenny came in," he said. "By the time we could get another one—you see what I mean? What chance would we have of finding them?"

"How about calling the cops?" Chip asked helpfully.

"What would we tell them? We don't know a crime's been committed, do we?"

"As far as we know it hasn't," Chip said.

"Maybe we ought to call a cab at that. We can cruise around and see what turns up."

But when they went inside to telephone, Mrs. Wilson walked briskly toward them. "Your father called, not more than five minutes ago."

"Aw," Chip said disappointedly. "I wish we'd have been here."

"He phoned from Puerto Rico," Mrs. Wilson said. "The operator told me he'd call back."

"When?" Jack asked quickly.

"All she said was that he would call back."

The phone rang. As Mrs. Wilson hurried to it, she said, "Maybe that's he now."

The boys walked toward the phone. But they stopped when Mrs. Wilson shook her head. The call wasn't for them.

They wandered aimlessly out onto the screened porch. The only thing they could do now, they decided, was to wait for their father's call.

"You know, Chip," Jack said, "I doubt if we'd have accomplished much anyhow by cruising around in a cab."

"I just hope Bob's okay."

"You know, when he hurried out of the restaurant," Jack said thoughtfully, "that wasn't just panic. He had reason to be scared of that cousin of his."

"All Lenny's got to do is keep Bob from diving. If he can do that till September seventh, then according to the will—"

"He'd never try anything that obvious." Jack shook his head. "It'd just get him in trouble."

There was grilled swordfish steak and pecan pie for dinner. But the boys didn't enjoy the meal. They were watching for Lenny and Bob, and also anticipating the call from their father. During the meal they remarked that they hadn't seen Crossland around, that he probably was no longer at the guesthouse. They agreed that this was a relief.

Back in their room Chip said, "How long do you have to wait before reporting somebody missing?"

"Did you hear that?" Jack whispered excitedly.

"What?"

Jack stood very still, trying hard to locate the source of the sound he had heard.

Simultaneously both boys saw Bob's face at the window. They hurried to it. As soon as they had opened the window for him, Bob climbed through. "What happened?" Chip asked eagerly. "Did he hold you prisoner?"

"You okay?" Jack asked.

"Why did you have to come in here through the

window?" Chip wanted to know.

"I got away from him." Bob moved about nervously. "But if Lenny's not already here, he'll be here soon."

The sudden ring of the phone startled the boys. Then Jack and Chip, realizing this must be the call from their father, lunged for the phone. Their race proved a dead heat. After a brief tug of war, Jack wrenched the phone from Chip.

"Hello," Jack said, a little out of breath. Looking up, he told Chip, "It's Dad, all right. I can hear them making the—" He broke off and, as he listened, a smile grew on his face. "Dad. . . . Yeah, yeah, this is Jack. . . . There's a little buzzing sound, but I can hear you all right. How are you? . . . Oh, everything's under control here. . . . No, no, we're not bored. . . . We haven't gotten around to taking those pictures yet. . . . Nothing's wrong. We've been so lazy, we just haven't gotten around to it. . . ."

Jack turned the phone over to Chip. Chip, too, assured his father that everything was under control. As he was winding up his conversation, there was a knock at the door.

"I bet it's Lenny," Bob said, looking about frantically.

"Get in there," Jack ordered, pointing to a closet.

There was another knock at the door as Bob raced to the closet.

Jack paused to compose himself before going to the door. As he moved forward Chip said on the phone, "Golly, Dad, why are you worried? You know Bermuda. It's peaceful as—"

Jack opened the door. When he saw it was Lenny he didn't open the door all the way. Lenny asked if he had seen Bob, and Jack shook his head.

"Okay. Thanks." Lenny turned away.

Chip had already hung up when Jack closed the door and came back into the room.

"Got rid of him," Jack whispered gleefully.

"Was it Lenny?" Chip asked.

Jack nodded, still happy over having outwitted Lenny. He moved toward the closet door, plainly to tell Bob that he could come out now that the coast was clear.

Before he reached the closet, the door of the room flew open and Lenny barged in. "Excuse me, fellows," he said, grinning. He looked around the room. To cover his obvious search of some sign of Bob, he said, "Your room's about the size of mine. I find it a little small, don't you?"

The boys just stared at Lenny wordlessly.

Lenny went on in his talkative way, "When you see Bob—if and when you see him—tell him he ought to learn to take a joke. I didn't mean to abduct him. I just grabbed him to show him a good time. I guess he told you about this deadline of his. But he's going at the whole thing too desperately. If he's not going to have fun now, when is he going to have it? . . ."

The boys continued to stare. They didn't even try to get a word in.

"But that's Bob for you. That doesn't mean"—Lenny pointed a finger at them—"that I don't think he's a real nice guy. Okay, if you see him before I do, you tell him what I said." Lenny paused after opening the door. He stood holding the doorknob. "I'll tell you something. Bob's my first cousin. And you know, he gives me the impression he's scared of me."

After Lenny had gone, Chip locked the door behind

him and then opened the closet.

The first thing Bob said was, "I *am* scared of him. No wonder he got that impression."

"Did you hear the rest of what he said?" Jack asked.

"All that about wanting to show me a good time," Bob replied, shaking his head in disgust. "I don't believe it. He acted like it was all a big joke, the way he grabbed me and all, but I'm not so sure it was. There's something else I'm not sure about. According to him, his mother sent him to kind of keep an eye on me. Aunt Evelyn's swell. She's the kind who would be worried about me. It's just that I suspect Lenny. And it's not exactly in the way I was bothered by Crossland. It's worse."

"Say," Chip said. "With Lenny on the prowl, maybe we had better not waste time."

"You mean dive now—at night?" Jack asked.

"It's been done, hasn't it?"

"Sure, Chip. It's been done. But not by us."

"Do you think we can do it?" Bob asked eagerly. "I'm all for it."

Suddenly Chip became very excited by the idea of

taking movies of life beneath the ocean at night.

In order to avoid meeting Lenny, the boys sneaked out the window. Walking to Hamilton, they found, wasn't too bad when there was an exciting adventure ahead.

But when they awakened Samson at the dock and told him what they had in mind, he shook his head vigorously.

"Why not?" Chip asked. "Night dives have been made before."

"Sharks," Samson said thoughtfully, rubbing his unshaven chin.

"What about sharks?" Chip asked.

Samson took a long time in answering. There was the sound of sandpaper as he continued to rub the stubble of his beard. "They feed at night, sharks do," he finally said. "They're night feeders."

15 *Danger Down Below*

"Do you know that to be a fact," Jack asked, "that sharks feed at night?"

Samson made a grunting sound and nodded.

"Well," Jack said to Chip and Bob, "what'll we do?"

Having nothing more to say, Samson turned away.

The boys and Bob moved closer together and talked in low tones.

Chip said that he knew his father would never pass up a chance to get interesting and important pictures. To do that would be against the code of a photojournalist.

"Besides," Chip said, "you remember what Crossland said that day? He said there aren't any sharks around here."

"Crossland," Jack said disparagingly. "I can't forget the way he seemed to want to scare Bob."

"No matter what you think of the guy," Chip objected, "he still might know something about sharks."

"Okay," Jack conceded. "Even if there are sharks around and even if they do feed at night, we might not meet up with one. After all, it's a big ocean."

Bob hadn't said anything. Without putting it in words, Jack and Chip asked for his opinion merely by looking at him and waiting.

"I'm for taking the chance," Bob said finally. "With Lenny down here I've just got to get it over with."

The three walked toward Samson, who stood silhouetted against the moonlight reflected from the water.

Jack made clear what they had decided. He did it by simply handing Samson the sketch that Reynolds had made of the *Texas Queen's* location. The skipper looked from the paper to the three boys, then shrugged his shoulders as if their recklessness was really no concern of his.

On the trip out, Bob was not only excited but in good spirits. He showed Jack and Chip a key he wore around his neck.

"This key will open a footlocker," he said. "The figurine's in it. I know you want to get some pictures, Chip. But it's that figurine I want."

"Don't build up your hopes, Bob," Jack warned.

"Oh, I know I might not get it tonight," Bob answered. It was clear by his excitement, however, that he was expecting to.

This time Samson didn't even check the improvised chart Jack had given him. He suddenly turned off the motor, threw the anchor overboard, and by his silence implied that he had done his job and the rest was up to them.

For light, each of the boys fastened a watertight flashlight to his head. Each had a knife in a sheath on his diving belt, also.

Just before going down the ladder into the water, Jack said, "Remember, this time nobody wanders off. Stick close together—no matter what."

The moon gave a pleasing, luminous glow to the

water. As before, they used the anchor line, descending single file. Chip carried the camera; it was torpedo shaped and had its own light.

The pleasant moonlight faded as they went deeper and deeper. The night waters had their own special, ominous quality which was not present during the day. At times the ocean appeared to be burning because of the luminous red wake of swimming worms and jelly-fish.

The bubbles rising from Bob, middleman on the anchor line, were observed carefully by Jack, who was above him. The increased number of bubbles meant that Bob was breathing faster than normal—and that meant he was scared.

He saw Bob let go of the anchor line and head for the surface. Bob was going so fast that he passed his bubbles, which was dangerous. Jack knew that any ascent faster than a foot a second could injure the lungs. Therefore he left the anchor line and intercepted Bob. He shoved at Bob in an attempt to stop him and get him to go back down in the water.

By this time Chip noticed the struggle going on above

him and rose to help Jack. Just as he was trying to grab one of Bob's threshing legs, his flashlight was kicked from his head. It sank to the bottom.

Finally the boys calmed Bob. After they had made it back to the anchor line, they saw the light from Chip's flashlight, just a few feet below them. This meant that they had practically reached the ocean floor.

They descended to the spot where the flashlight lay. As Chip picked it up and began to fasten it on his head, he noticed that both Jack and Bob were motioning and pointing wildly. It was then that Chip saw that the beam from his flashlight had illumined the *Texas Queen*. The name of the yacht, in big letters, was plainly visible on the looming hull.

When Chip finished making his flashlight secure, he began to film the approach of Jack and Bob to the sunken yacht. He lay in a horizontal position with the camera extended before him.

Suddenly a giant manta ray swooped between the boys and the yacht. Its fins moved like immense black wings.

Chip continued to shoot the action in front of him.

TEXAS QUEEN

Jack and Bob were rising in an attempt to escape from the sea monster, which swooped about as though searching for a chance to strike.

Chip stood his ground, even as the ray zoomed straight at him. An instant before collision, the ray swooped upward. Chip headed quickly for the surface. He caught up with Jack and Bob, who were holding onto the anchor line and waiting for him.

It wasn't until then that Chip realized that he had dropped the camera in the excitement of escaping from the manta ray. With only motions as a means of communication, Chip futilely tried to tell them what had happened.

All Jack did was to point upward, signaling that they should surface.

Stubbornly Chip pointed down. Manta ray, shark, killer whale—no matter what—he was heading back down to get the camera and the pictures he'd taken.

16 *Chip Chips In*

Jack descended with Chip. The manta ray was no longer in sight. Chip spotted the camera immediately and went straight for it.

A few minutes later, when they were all back on the *For Keeps,* Chip said, "The way I found the camera seemed too easy. I just had the feeling something awful was due to happen before I made it up to the surface."

"Golly, hasn't enough happened to satisfy you?" Jack asked sharply.

"I'm sorry," Bob said. "The way I panicked again—no excuse for it."

Samson, who had been standing idly nearby, asked

laconically, "Ready to go back?"

Jack nodded. "We're not doing any more diving tonight, are we, fellows?"

"I know I'm not," Chip said.

"I don't blame you, Chip, for feeling that way," Bob said glumly. "I acted like a first-rate kook."

"What are you talking about?" Chip said. "No matter what happened tonight, I wouldn't want to do any more diving. I'm going to have dreams about that ray. Jack, how wide do you think that thing was?"

Jack had just finished helping Samson weigh anchor. "You mean the ray?" he said. "Big or little, those rays are harmless."

"Are you kidding?" Chip said in disbelief.

"Well, they've never been known to hurt a diver."

"Don't tell me that ray just wanted to play tag. Why, it dived at me like it was going to smash me flatter than—"

"But it didn't hurt you," Jack reminded Chip.

"I know why you're saying all this," Chip said. "You don't want to give me a bravery medal for going back after the camera."

Samson was steering straight across the moonlit water, heading directly for the harbor in Hamilton. Bob sat silent and thoughtful.

"Fellows," Bob said all of a sudden, "I know now why I panicked. Remember, Jack, what you said before you gave me my first lesson? You said the ocean was like a burning building. Now it comes back to me. That's the feeling I had. All that luminous stuff underwater made me think of fire. And the water seemed like smoke to me. I felt like I was trapped and suffocating."

"You're not the only one," Chip said. "It was weird, that's for sure."

"We've found the *Texas Queen,* that's one thing," Bob observed thankfully.

"I can't wait to see what I got on my film," Chip said.

When they arrived in the harbor, however, Jack and Bob thought it was a good idea to stay overnight on the *For Keeps.* Chip didn't think so.

"We don't want to run into Lenny, do we?" Jack argued.

"And, Chip," Bob said pleadingly, "it will give us a

chance to get an early start tomorrow morning. Maybe we'll be able to miss the tourist divers—you know, around the other wrecks."

"But I want to develop this film," Chip insisted.

"You're acting like a kid," Jack said. "If you're scared of that ray, you don't have to dive tomorrow."

"Did I say anything about being scared?" Chip snapped.

"You were sure impressed by the size of that ray," Jack answered.

Chip turned on Bob. "All I said— Now, isn't this right, Bob? I didn't say anything about that ray. All I said— Now, wait a minute, Jack, give me a chance to finish. I didn't say anything about a ray. All I said was that I wanted to develop my film."

Chip got off the boat as soon as it docked.

"Don't go away sore," Jack called to him.

"Who's sore?" Chip snapped.

"We'll wait for you tomorrow," Bob shouted as Chip walked away. "We want you to dive with us."

Chip turned and made a waving gesture with his arm. "No, no, you go ahead!" he yelled back. "You ask

Jack. He'll tell you! I'm scared of that ray!"

The next morning Jack and Bob dived. Everything went smoothly. First they circled the *Texas Queen*. It was an exploring, cautious maneuver. The deck of the yacht slanted at a forty-five-degree angle, but this didn't present a problem, for they simply floated over the deck. But they found they couldn't get to the footlocker that contained the figurine, for a hatch that was jammed barred their way. They tried singly and together to open the hatch, but each time without success.

When they surfaced they were surprised to find Chip aboard the *For Keeps*.

"See that boat out there?" Chip said, pointing off in the distance. "I got a lift on her. It's a skin-diving tour. She's got ten divers aboard, all of them out to take a look at the wrecks."

Jack studied Chip. "That's not what you're excited about. I can tell something's up by the way you—"

"How did the dive go?" Chip interrupted innocently.

Bob started to tell Chip about the jammed hatch, but Jack broke in. "Come on, Chip," he said, "tell us first what's got you all excited."

"You didn't think my going off last night was so important, did you?" Chip accused.

"You still sore?" Jack asked. "Is that why you're stalling?"

Chip smiled. "What were you saying, Bob?" he asked, trying to needle Jack. "You got down to the *Texas Queen. . . .*"

"Yeah," Jack answered quickly, irritably. "But a jammed hatch kept us from going below. Okay. Now, Chip, it's your turn to talk."

Chip shrugged. "I want you to see the pictures I took yesterday," he said.

"Did you develop them?" Jack asked, surprised.

"Yeah," Chip said. "It was black and white. And I developed just the little I'd exposed, using one of those 'flop tests' that Dad makes. I rented a projector—in Hamilton. Oh, are you going to get a blast when you see what I have on that film!"

"Well, tell us," Jack urged impatiently.

"No, no," Chip said, shaking his head. "I better not."

"Why?" Jack asked. "Because you got sore last night?"

"Listen, Jack, I just don't want to tell you all about

the pictures ahead of time. If I did, you might see things that aren't really there. I don't want to go putting ideas into your head. It's much too important."

When the boys returned to the guesthouse Chip had the projector and screen all set up in their room. The slats of the Venetian blinds were closed. Jack turned off the lights as soon as Chip flipped on the projector. The room wasn't really long enough, so the picture overflowed the screen onto the wall.

At first there was just a shot of water. Soon, across the upper half of the picture, a pair of legs and a pair of fin-encased feet floated by.

"I wonder who those belonged to," Jack laughed.

Next Jack and Bob appeared, swimming toward the background of the screen.

"Good," Jack said. "This is getting better now."

"How about watching?" Chip asked irritably.

Jack and Bob were now drifting apart on the screen.

"When the ray shows up," Jack said, "is that when we get the blast you were talking about?"

Chip didn't answer.

The hull of the *Texas Queen* could now be seen on

the screen. Suddenly the ray, looking like a pancake-shaped cloud, swooped downward. The agitation of the water obscured everything for a long moment. Then the ray came zooming right at the audience, filling the entire screen.

"That does it," Chip said as he stopped the film and flipped off the projector.

Jack immediately turned on the lights.

"Not bad, Chip," Jack said. "But you gave it too much of a buildup."

Bob said, "The shot of the ray. That's the best part, don't you think?"

"I don't want to say anything yet," Chip told Bob.

"Why not?" Jack said. "The show's over, isn't it?"

"Turn off the lights again, will you, Jack?"

"You mean it's not over?" Jack asked in surprise.

Chip ran the film in reverse. He stopped the film at a frame which showed a close-up of the ray.

The ray was wearing a diver's mask!

"It's not a ray!" Jack exclaimed. "Do you see that, Bob! It's a diver, just dressed up in a costume with black wings!"

17 *"The Name Is Familiar...."*

Jack hurried up close to the screen. "You think it's Lenny?" he asked excitedly.

He moved back again, discovering that a position too close to the screen made his view worse rather than better.

Bob and the boys studied the picture, which was halted in mid-action on the screen.

"It's hard to be sure," Jack said slowly. "All you've got are eyes, nose—and a little bit of forehead."

"And the faceplate," Chip observed, "keeps you from getting a good view of whoever it is."

"Wouldn't surprise me if it's Lenny," Bob said. "It's

the kind of a whacky thing he'd go in for."

"But it could be anybody—even that big brag Crossland," Jack mused. "Though I can't see why *he'd*—"

They pulled up the blinds, turned off the lights, rolled up the screen, and put the projector in its case. Throughout all this activity, they were thoughtfully silent.

With nothing left to do, Jack paced around the room, running his hand over his red hair. Chip and Bob stood watching him, as though depending on his coming up with some brilliant idea.

When he stopped pacing, Bob and Chip tensed with expectation.

"It's pretty plain," Jack said, more to himself than to the boys, "that someone is trying to keep us away from the *Texas Queen*."

"Well, who doesn't know that?" Chip said, with both rebuke and disappointment.

"But there's no question of it now," Jack pointed out.

Bob nodded. "Your brother's right."

"Up to now, we didn't know—for sure," Jack

went on. "The chart was swiped and it was changed, but that might have been done for other reasons. But this new development, well, it changes the whole picture."

"Lenny might have tried to get the figurine," Bob suggested. "He would have run into the same trouble we did. So he dressed up in this manta-ray rig to scare us away, wanting to be sure *we* didn't get it."

Jack nodded. "And Lenny's the only one—that we know—who's got a motive."

"I know what we ought to do," Chip said, snapping his fingers hard, his eyes bright with sudden excitement.

"What?" both Bob and Jack asked.

"Have a showdown with Lenny, that's what," Chip answered.

"You mean come right out and tell him—"

"Yeah," Chip cut in on Jack. "That's right. Tell him we know he swiped the chart and dressed up like a ray—and—and everything."

"But if we're wrong . . ." Bob said hesitantly.

"We'll get a reaction out of him, won't we?" Chip asked. "If he's guilty, he'll give himself away. It will show. We'll be able to tell."

"Chip's got something there," Jack admitted.

A scratching started at the door, then a whining.

"Is that Blaze?" Jack asked. "What's he doing here? I tied him up good and tight."

Chip went to the door and opened it.

Lenny stood there, a wide grin on his face. He was wearing white shorts and a white shirt, dressed for tennis. "Did I hear something about your tying me up?" he asked. "I just saw the Dalmatian around back. They told me that spotted hound was yours. And so I thought I'd do a takeoff on him, just for laughs."

Jack, Chip, and Bob were speechless. Confronted by Lenny so suddenly, they didn't know how to start accusing him as they had planned.

"Why did you take that powder on me?" Lenny asked Bob. Without giving his cousin a chance to answer, he went on, "I've got a real surprise for you. You'll never guess who else trailed you down to Bermuda. Come on, I have him waiting out here. I just wanted to prepare you ahead of time."

"Who is it?" Bob asked as they all went out the door.

"I told you that Ma sent me here to keep an eye

on you," Lenny said irrelevantly. "And when I saw him—I bumped into him right on Front Street. Maule's not the sort to get embarrassed, but seeing me seemed to shake him up."

"Maule?" Bob said, puzzled. "The name's familiar but—"

"Think a little," Lenny said. "You'll remember who he is. Stanley Maule. He actually acted like I'd caught him in the act."

They had stopped in front of the registration desk.

"Okay, I've kept you in suspense long enough." Lenny made them all draw up close to him. Then he said to Bob, "He's executor of your father's estate."

"Oh, yes," Bob said. "Maule. I remember now. Sure."

"Before we go out and see him," Lenny said, "I want to put you on your guard. This Maule's a slick operator. Personally, I think he's up to something. His base of operations is New York. So what's he doing down here? And at this time? That's what makes me suspicious. You've never met him, have you?" he asked Bob. "I'm telling you, he's a ruthless kind of guy. Just be on your guard. Okay?"

The boys stopped short in amazement when they were still a distance from the man who waited outside.

Lenny stopped ahead of them. Turning around, he asked what was the matter.

"Why, that's Crossland!" Chip exclaimed.

"It sure is," Jack said. "The great authority on sharks."

"What are you guys talking about?" Lenny said. "That's Stanley Maule—in person."

Jack shrugged. "Could be," he said. "But he used the name Crossland when he was living here."

"Well, Bob Jillman," Maule said as he came toward Bob with an outstretched hand. He shook Bob's hand and slapped him on the shoulder. "I take it Lenny has revealed my true identity by this time?"

"That I did," Lenny said, answering for Bob. "I've got to go now. Give you a chance to talk. I'm late." He glanced at his wristwatch. "I've a tennis appointment."

Lenny dashed off, and the boys and Bob were left alone with Maule. Even though Maule was now wearing Bermuda shorts and knee-length socks, he still gave the impression of being a coach or a former professional football player. He was big and well-built. And his nose had obviously once been broken—undoubtedly in a game. And he still rubbed them the wrong way.

Maule brushed aside Bob's introductions of Jack and Chip.

"Of course I know Red and his brother," Maule said. "We broke bread together at many a meal. How are you, Red?"

"My name's Jack," Jack corrected him, in a tone of voice that made it plain he didn't like to be called Red.

"I don't understand, Mr. Maule," Bob said, speaking with some belligerence, too, "why you haven't spoken to me before now."

Chip spoke up then. "I'm Chip Power." That he had felt ignored up to this point was strongly implied.

Maule smiled, as though to say that all this hostility didn't bother him. He explained that he hadn't told them he was the administrator of the Jillman estate because he was afraid that if Bob knew who he was, it might add to the pressure of the deadline. This was also why he had used the fictitious name Crossland. When Lenny, who knew him, arrived, he had moved to another guesthouse. He went on to explain that he had come to Bermuda for two reasons. First of all, he wanted to keep informed of the progress Bob was making toward meeting the deadline of the will. And, second, by being right on the scene he could extend the deadline by the one and a half hours it would take Bob to fly jet from Bermuda to New York with the figurine.

"How are things going?" Maule asked.

Taking Bob by the arm, he began to stroll with him across the lawn. After a few steps he turned and invited Jack and Chip to come along with them.

As the brothers walked behind Maule and Bob, they heard Bob tell how they had been attacked by the phony manta ray. Obviously the boy was satisfied with Maule's explanation of his presence in Bermuda and was anxious to confide in him.

"You think we ought to tell him," Chip whispered to Jack, "how we suspect Lenny?"

Jack shook his head and murmured, "No. Absolutely not. Bob *wants* to trust him, I guess—mostly because Lenny warned him against the guy. I say, *go slow.*"

By this time Bob had also told Maule that the chart had been stolen and altered.

The big man stopped. When they were grouped around him he said, "I'm astounded by all this. And I'm certainly going to look into this ray business and the theft of the chart."

"Are you really?" Chip said dubiously.

"Of course I am," Maule answered at once. "You sound as though you distrust me. I want you to understand as clearly and perfectly as possible"—he struck his fist into the palm of his hand for emphasis—"that I'm here for just one reason—to help Bob. I tried to persuade his father not to put that stipulation in the will about recovering the figurine. But it *is* in the will—and so I'm out rooting for Bob to come through. I'm not an executor *de son tort*. I'm the rightful, lawfully authorized executor. As such, Bob, I'd like to see this provision of the will carried out, not only because it is in the document but because this is what was in the mind and heart of your late, beloved father—that you be his heir."

The boys stood speechless after that outburst.

Maule looked about surreptitiously, then whispered

that they should move along with him, that he wanted to be farther away from the house.

"What's the matter?" Chip asked.

"It's about Lenny," Maule whispered. "Let's wait till we get over to those trees."

When they approached the edge of the lawn Maule stopped. "Bob, I know Lenny is your cousin," he said. "But how do you honestly feel about him?"

Bob shrugged.

"I take that to mean you're not too attached to him," Maule said. "Good! I have a very strong suspicion that he hasn't come to Bermuda just to play tennis. As your father's executor I'm warning you—watch him! He's a sly, dangerous article!"

18 *Jack's Solution*

Just then a cab arrived. Maule complained because it had been so long in coming.

"It must be almost an hour since I called for it," he said irritably. "But it did give me time to have this talk with you, Bob, and with you, Red. I'm sorry, I meant Jack. And with you—" He tried to remember Chip's name, but he couldn't.

"Chip," Chip said grudgingly.

"Chip," Maule echoed. "Chip. Of course."

After the cab pulled away, Bob and the boys started walking idly away from the guesthouse.

"Wait a minute," Jack said. "I just thought of the

way Lenny scratched at our door. Blaze has been tied up a lot lately. He ought to have a run."

Bob and Chip remained on the lawn, waiting for Jack to come back with the dog.

"What do you think of Maule?" Bob asked curiously.

"What Lenny said about him might be right. You know, about his being a—"

"Oh, I disagree," Bob said. "Would a sharp operator forget your name, the way he did?"

"And he called Jack, Red. That wasn't smart. Still he looks like a wheeler-dealer to me."

Blaze tore across the lawn. He was racing Jack and was now far ahead of him. He barked and leaped high in the air when he reached Bob and Chip, then ran on ahead as the boys strolled down toward the beach.

"What do *you* think?" Chip said to Jack. "Does Maule strike you as a crook?"

"Well, I certainly didn't trust him when he started talking," Jack answered. "But, actually, the guy has no motive for causing trouble. What's he to gain from the will?"

"Maybe there's a motive we don't know about."

"True," Jack admitted. "True. But we *know* Lenny has got a motive. And, gosh, Maule sure did warn us about him. You heard him."

"Yeah, sure," Chip said. "And Lenny warned us about Maule. So where does that leave us?"

They stopped at the water's edge. Blaze wasn't in sight, having run off on a side trail.

"You know what I think?" Bob said, breaking a long silence. "We ought to just forget about both of them. I—I know what I have to do. I've got to dive and get that figurine. The time's short. The seventh isn't very far off. And right now, we're stuck."

"That's for sure," Chip agreed with a mirthless laugh. "We're stuck every bit as much as that hatch is."

On their way to the diving spot the next morning, three sailing boats crossed the bow of the *For Keeps*. They were all Bermuda-fitted dinghies.

"Hey!" Chip exclaimed. "That's supposed to be good luck, boats passing that way!"

"I hope so," Bob said fervently.

It seemed all of five minutes before Samson turned from the wheel and commented on the sailing boats.

"*Bad* luck," he said, his mouth turned down in a frown.

As soon as Samson's back was turned, Bob hissed at Jack and Chip, "Let's not start going in for witchcraft. I'm getting that figurine. Period. And that's final."

Bob's determination seemed to work, too. With the crowbar they had taken with them on their dive, they were able to pry up the hatch.

Bob gestured that he was going below. He pointed to the key on a chain around his neck. The bubbles came faster from his lung, but this time it was from excitement and not from fear.

The boys tried to give Bob a hand as he went down through the hatch. After he had made it into the passageway below, he moved backward. Both Jack and Chip hung onto the hatchway opening, peering down at Bob. They watched as he fitted his key into a large footlocker on the starboard side of the passageway.

After a time, he turned. Looking up at Jack and Chip, he shook his head. He made a wide gesture with both hands, clearly indicating his helplessness.

Chip immediately made his way through the hatch.

Now Jack alone stared down, watching Bob and

Chip. He saw Bob once again try unsuccessfully to unlock the footlocker. Then Chip tried turning the key. Frustrated, Chip tried lifting the lid of the footlocker, even though he knew it was still locked.

Jack handed down the crowbar. First Bob and then Chip tried to open the footlocker with it, but neither had any luck. Finally the boys quit in despair.

There was grim silence all during the trip back to shore that afternoon.

In the evening, after dinner, Bob was in Jack's and Chip's room when the telephone rang.

"Must be Dad!" Chip cried out as he grabbed the phone.

But the call was from Maule. He reported that Lenny had not been the phony manta ray. Some valuable items had been found on a wreck not too far from the *Texas Queen*. The disguise had been used to frighten away amateur divers, while the man who found the treasure had time to look for more.

"I still don't have word for you on the chart," Maule told Chip. "For the time being, you had better assume Lenny was behind the theft and the—the rest of it."

When Chip relayed Maule's information to Jack and Bob, they were unable to agree on its significance.

"For the first time," Jack said, "the guy seems unquestionably on the level."

"How do you figure that?" Chip asked curiously.

"Look, if he were just out to make Lenny seem as guilty as possible, would he have cleared him the way he did? No. He would let us go on thinking he was that phony manta ray."

"Right," Bob said.

"So it looks like Lenny is the guy we really have to watch," Chip said.

"That's exactly what Maule said," Jack pointed out.

They were drinking Cokes when Chip suggested they salvage the *Texas Queen*.

"I heard of a boat being raised with inner tubes," he went on to explain. "You take a whole lot of tubes down and attach 'em all the way around the boat you're bringing up. Fill them up with compressed air. Of course, you have to take air tanks down along with the tubes."

"Sounds like a project," Jack said dubiously.

Bob didn't like the idea, either. He shook his head. "I'd love to see the boat afloat again," he said, "but we don't have the time to do anything like that."

Jack jumped up. "Wow!" he exclaimed. "Have I got an idea!"

Bob and Chip stood up and closed in on Jack, eager to learn what it was.

Jack finished off his Coke and put his bottle down, still not telling them anything. He began searching for a classified telephone directory.

"Forget the phone book," Jack said, after Bob and Chip had joined in the search. "I just wanted to see if there was a locksmith around. There surely must be."

"Oh!" Chip said. "Oh, I get it. But you'll have to find a locksmith who's a diver, too."

"I didn't mean that he would go down to the *Texas Queen* to do the job," Jack said. "Why not bring the locker up? With inner tubes. That would be a breeze, compared with floating a whole boat."

"Great!" Bob exclaimed.

But in the midst of their excitement over the idea, Jack suddenly held up his hand. "Shhh!" he warned.

They stood perfectly still, listening intently.

"I'm sure I heard someone at the door," Jack said.

Impulsively Chip rushed forward and jerked open the door.

"Nobody," he said, looking up and down the hall.

Jack came to see for himself; he was sure he had heard a noise. He bent down and picked up something that had been leaning against the wall. It was a tennis racket in a press.

"Hey," Chip said when Jack came back into the room. "Lenny plays tennis."

"And this is his racket, too," Jack said. "His name's printed right here on the press. I knew somebody was out there. I was sure I heard somebody."

Bob said, "He put the racket down when he—"

"Yeah. Yeah." Jack nodded. "You would naturally do that if you were going to put your ear flat up against a door to listen."

"So he knows we're going to bring up the footlocker," Chip said glumly. "What's he going to do about it? Is he going to try to stop us?"

"It's hard to say," Jack answered. "But he might!"

19 *Success—and Failure*

The next morning they had a little trouble in prying the footlocker free. However, as soon as they attached the inner tubes to it and inflated them, the footlocker shot right to the surface.

To avoid an air embolism, the boys had to ascend considerably slower than the footlocker. They left the anchor line when Jack spotted the oblong shape of the locker and pointed to it. Another shape was shadowing the water, and they had to be careful not to come up under it.

Alongside the footlocker, which was surrounded by its supporting inner tubes, the boys saw a dinghy. It had been the dinghy's hull which they had seen from below the surface. There were four men in it. All looked alike, wearing swimming trunks and domino masks. Two of them, however, held spear guns—which were aimed downward at Bob, Jack, and Chip in the water.

One of the men holding a spear gun snarled, "I wouldn't cause any trouble, frogmen, if I was you."

Chip pulled off his mask and spit out his mouthpiece. "Bob," he shouted, "they're stealing your footlocker!"

"Move," the man who had spoken before ordered, "unless you want a taste of one of these spears!"

"Did Lenny hire you to do this?" Chip shouted.

This time Chip didn't get an answer. One of the men in the dinghy was down on his knees, reaching far out with the arm that held the dagger. He was deflating the inner tubes by stabbing holes in them. Two others—one at each end of the footlocker—were wrestling the locker aboard the dinghy.

Jack led the way to the *For Keeps,* going as fast as he could. He obviously wanted to pursue the dinghy. Bob and Chip swam after him.

When Samson was instructed to chase the dinghy that had the footlocker aboard, he made no comment. But he put down his bottle of orange soda with obvious reluctance.

Clouds as white as the sail of the dinghy scudded across the peaceful blue sky.

Samson had the throttle all the way forward as he headed straight for the other boat. Jack, Chip, and Bob huddled near Samson, staring through the windshield.

"What'll we do if we catch her?" Chip asked anxiously. "They have those spear guns."

Jack and Bob didn't speak. They had no answer.

"We're gaining on her!" Bob exclaimed suddenly.

"Are we?" Jack said dubiously. "That's a strong wind she's got. And she's carrying an awful lot of sail."

Suddenly the motor of the *For Keeps* went dead. Instead of its roar, there was just the whispering, lulling sound of the water.

"Oh, no!" Chip wailed. "Not a breakdown! Not now!"

"Sounds like we're out of gas," Bob said.

Instead of speaking, Samson went to the gas tank—

a double tank—and switched the line from the empty tank to the full one.

Chip shouted, "Hurrah!" when the motor started up again. But his cry died on his lips.

Looking over the water, the boys now saw two dinghies instead of one. The new arrival was yellow.

"Just keep your eye on the dinghy that's painted red," Jack instructed. "She's ours."

"Can't you go any faster?" Bob asked Samson.

Samson didn't act as if he had heard the question.

"He's got the throttle all the way forward," Jack told Bob.

"We've got to stay on their tail," Bob said. "That will keep them from dumping the locker. They don't want us around when they do that."

The horn of the *For Keeps* sounded. It had the bawling sound of a cow with a bad cold. Dinghies were suddenly coming from all directions. Each hull seemed a different color: red, yellow, brown, white, turquoise.

Samson pulled back the throttle and jabbed the horn's button with his thumb.

"Been in a race," Samson said, by way of explanation.

"You mean all those dinghies?" Bob asked.

"Race is over." Samson had suddenly become talkative. "They're heading for Hamilton."

"Ours is the red one," Jack reminded everyone. "Keep your eye on her."

"Jack!" Bob exclaimed agonizingly. "There are three red ones! Don't you see three?"

"Well, that's the one," Jack said, pointing to one of the red dinghies.

"No!" Bob said. "Over there, over there!" He, too, pointed. "The one they're bailing water out of. The wind has got her skimming along on her gunwales."

Chip didn't agree with either Bob or his brother. The red dinghy they hadn't pointed out was the one he thought they ought to follow.

One of the red dinghies separated itself from the others. Without asking whether or not he should, Samson followed her.

"Do you have binoculars?" Jack shouted to Samson after a few moments.

Without a word Samson lifted up a seat board and produced a powerful pair.

Jack trained the glasses on the dinghy, then focused them. He began to shake his head almost at once. "We goofed!" he cried. He handed the binoculars to Bob. "Go ahead. You want to take a look?"

"There's a girl!" Bob exclaimed with surprise as he used the binoculars. "A blond girl is on that dinghy!"

"You don't see the footlocker, do you?" Jack said bitterly. "We had one chance in three of picking the right dinghy. And what did we do? We flubbed it."

On the way back to Hamilton, they tried hard to locate the other red dinghies, but they had vanished.

"We should have used these things earlier," Jack said glumly.

"They're sure no good to us now," Chip agreed. "That's for sure. By now Lenny has dumped that footlocker out in the ocean—"

"Oh, we set it up nice for him," Bob said, even more depressed than Chip and Jack. "He let us do all the work. He's clever. We got the footlocker up for him. We handed it over. You're right, Chip, by now he's dumped it in the ocean. I'm licked! What can I do now, fellows? There's absolutely nothing I can do!"

20 *A Misunderstanding*

After the *For Keeps* docked, Bob paid Samson the money he owed him for his services and the use of the boat. It was a silent, solemn ritual. Paying Samson implied that the search for the figurine was over, and that Bob had been cut out of his father's will.

"Wait," Samson said as he stuffed the money into his pocket and moved away.

In a minute he returned with bottles of orange soda. He passed them out to the boys.

"Luck's funny," he said. He was making an awkward attempt to cheer them up. "It'll be back. Luck—it comes and goes."

They drank orange soda with no further conversation. Water lapping against the hull of the *For Keeps* made the only sound.

Samson took the bottle from his mouth. "Those three boats yesterday," he said. "Remember? Crossing our bow—"

"Yeah," Chip said. "I said that meant good luck. I was wrong. And how!"

"But luck's funny," Samson insisted. "Your luck could change."

They shook hands with Samson. After going up the cleated plank to the dock, the boys turned around. There stood Samson, holding an empty bottle, watching them. His immobility and his steady, impassive stare made him appear sinister.

They all felt it. To break the tension as they moved quickly on, Chip said, "The guy was trying to cheer us up, with that orange drink and all."

Bob turned on Chip furiously. "Was he?" he demanded. "You saw how he was standing there watching us like some kind of fiend. He brought us bad luck. I never heard that three boats crossing your bow was bad luck. But he had to say it was. And didn't he go chasing the wrong dinghy? Aw-w-w"—he swung his arm in a gesture of disgust—"what's the use of talking about it now?"

Jack and Chip didn't try to answer this outbreak; they were afraid of saying the wrong thing.

During the cab ride back to the guesthouse Bob suddenly spoke again, as though he were summing up his real feelings. "Samson's okay, I suppose," he said. "I didn't mean any of that stuff I said about him. If anybody's to blame, it's me."

"I wouldn't say that," Chip said. "After all—"

He broke off when Jack gave him a sharp poke in the ribs. He couldn't see where any more discussion was going to help.

The instant they entered the guesthouse, Mrs. Wilson called to Bob from the registration desk.

"Your aunt—Mrs. Thomas—is here," Mrs. Wilson said. "And she's—"

"Aunt Evelyn!" Bob exclaimed with disbelief.

"Yes." Mrs. Wilson nodded. "And she's been looking for you."

"Say," Chip said to Jack. "Aunt Evelyn. She's Lenny's mother, isn't she?"

"I'm not sure if your aunt went to her room," Mrs. Wilson said. "I'll ring for her, if you want me to. Shall I?"

"Oh, no, no, no!" Bob said, raising his hands quickly.

He immediately went into a whispered conference with Jack and Chip. He didn't want them to say anything to his aunt about what Lenny had done, he told the boys.

"It would break her heart," he told them. "And Aunt Evelyn's real swell."

"I won't say a thing," Jack promised.

"Me, neither," Chip said.

When they looked up they saw Lenny coming toward them. He was grinning. Blaze was with him.

"You look like you're in a huddle on the ten-yard line," Lenny said, still grinning.

It was obvious that the sight of his cousin's smile, coming at the end of a day of bitter disappointment, was too much for Bob. His face turned pale and he was breathing fast. Without a word he rushed at him, throwing an overhand punch with all his strength. Lenny stepped forward, causing the blow to go over his shoulder. The boys grabbed Bob and pulled him back.

"You deserve a lot more than a punch in the nose," Bob shouted at Lenny.

The excitement aroused Blaze, and he began to bark. People came from every direction to see what was going on.

"Would you tell me something, Bob?" Lenny said with infuriating calm. "Why would you want to punch me—a nice guy like me—in the nose?"

Bob tried to pull free of the hold the boys had on him. "You have the nerve," he shouted, "to ask me that, after what you did?"

"Bob, I didn't want to go snooping around, but—"

"Where did you dump it?" Bob demanded.

Chip turned to quiet Blaze. Just at that moment, Bob lunged forward and broke the grip Jack had on him. Bob and Lenny began to wrestle, locked tightly in each other's arms.

Spectators helped the boys pry Bob and Lenny apart. It was then that Mrs. Wilson and a tall, self-assured woman arrived.

"What's going on here?" the woman with Mrs. Wilson asked. "Why in the world are you two fighting?"

"Aunt Evelyn!" Bob exclaimed. "I didn't—"

Bob's aunt gave him a quick kiss on the cheek. "This is an odd way to welcome your aunt, I must say." She took his arm and started leading him away. There was an efficient practicality about her. "We should at least have a little privacy." She turned her head. "Lenny, please come along."

All of them—including Blaze—went out onto the lawn. A few witnesses to the fight also wandered outside, plainly hopeful that the excitement wasn't yet over.

"Lenny, I certainly didn't send you off to Bermuda," Aunt Evelyn said when they stopped, "to fight with your cousin."

"What did you mean before?" Lenny asked Bob. "Excuse me, Mother. It seems there was something I was supposed to have dumped."

Bob turned his head away. His tightly pressed lips indicated he was determined not to speak to Lenny.

"What's this quarrel about?" Bob's aunt said, getting right to the heart of the matter.

"All I can tell you, Mother," Lenny answered, "is that Bob thinks I did something I didn't do. Ask him what I'm supposed to have done. You can see he's mad at me. He's not talking—not to me."

"Pardon me—" Jack began.

Before he could go on, Lenny introduced him and Chip to his mother. "They've been helping Bob to get that figurine," he added.

"There's a misunderstanding here," Jack told Aunt Evelyn. "We've been suspicious of your son."

"We've been more than that," Chip said.

"Suspicious!" Bob's aunt exclaimed. "Of Lenny?"

"Aunt Evelyn," Bob said, "I didn't want to upset you. I thought I'd keep it from you—what Lenny did."

"What did I tell you?" Lenny said. "I'm supposed to have done something."

"It's all a misunderstanding," Jack persisted. "You didn't do it, Lenny. I know that now."

"Oh," Lenny said, grinning sarcastically. "I'm glad to hear that."

"Hey, Jack," Chip said, puzzled. "If Lenny didn't do it, do you know who did?"

"Of course," Jack said. "Don't you?"

"You mean Maule?" Chip asked, with an excited eagerness.

Aunt Evelyn gasped. "That's why I've come here, Bob," she said, "to warn you about that man."

"Why, Mother," Lenny said, "I did warn him. I told Bob and these fellows just what kind of a slippery character Maule is."

Aunt Evelyn went on to explain that ever since her brother's death, Maule had persisted in trying to persuade her to marry him. Because Bob's share in the estate would go to her if Bob failed to fulfill the stipulation of the will, Aunt Evelyn was sure that Maule wanted her to receive Bob's share so that marriage to her would be worthwhile. When she learned the conditions of the will and that Maule had gone to Bermuda, she immediately suspected that he was up to no good.

"That's why I sent Lenny immediately," she concluded. "I told him, Bob, that he was to help you in any way he could."

"I've got to confess I didn't do a very good job, Mother," Lenny said. "I like tennis better than I like snooping around." He turned to Bob. "What happened to the footlocker? How did you make out with it? I overheard you say—"

"Oh, we got it up," Bob said unhappily.

"And as soon as we did, Maule took it away from us," Jack added. "He and his men were all wearing masks. But the mask—they were those half things—didn't cover Maule's broken nose. I noticed it and thought there was something familiar about it. I didn't think any more about it. But when Bob talked about punching Lenny in the nose, it came to me in a flash that one of the crooks in that dinghy had to be Maule."

Bob immediately started apologizing to Lenny. Lenny didn't let him get very far, however, for he said he was off to play, not tennis this time, but cricket.

"Whale of a game, I understand," Lenny said. "Smashing! Well, when you're in Bermuda, you ought to do as the British do."

Jack and Chip were the next to leave, in order to give Bob a chance to talk to his aunt. They hadn't reached the guesthouse when Bob dashed by them.

Jack grabbed Bob by the arm. "What gives now?" he asked.

Aunt Evelyn was hurrying toward them, as though determined to stop Bob.

"I've just begun to fight!" Bob shouted. "I'm getting that Maule! I'm making him take me to where he dumped that locker!"

21 *Blaze Shows the Way*

Jack and Chip didn't rush after Bob as he hurried to the guesthouse; they were too dumbfounded by his show of reckless determination. A moment later Aunt Evelyn appeared, panting heavily from her unaccustomed run.

"Just take it easy," Jack said, offering her his arm.

"You were running too hard," Chip told her.

"We—we—we should stop Bob," Aunt Evelyn barely managed to tell them.

"It's okay," Jack said soothingly. "Don't worry."

But the assurance Bob's aunt seemed to have had before was gone now.

"I'm afraid," she sobbed, "something terrible might happen to Bob."

She made an effort to start running again, but the boys restrained her. After a moment she told them she had made Bob an offer. As soon as she received what would have been Bob's share in the estate, she was going to turn it over to him. But Bob wouldn't hear of this. Her offer renewed his determination to get the figurine, and prove his right to be the heir. He wanted more than ever to act in a way that would have made his father proud of him.

"Golly," Chip said, "you can't blame him, can you?"

They had started moving toward the guesthouse, Jack and Chip still holding onto Aunt Evelyn's arms. Suddenly she straightened and shrugged free of them.

"I'm all right now," she said, seeming like her old self again—practical, efficient, strong. "I've acted foolishly. Bob is doing the right thing. He's never been one to stand on his own two feet. What he's doing now is really wonderful."

"Just since we've known him he's changed a lot," Chip said.

"Let's see now," Aunt Evelyn said, getting down to business. "Maule may be on his boat."

"Has he got one?" Jack asked. "I didn't know that."

"Oh, my, yes," she said. "In quite a few of his proposals he spoke of his boat. We would sail away to an isle of bliss—*he* said. *Lady Fair* is the name of the boat. You tell Bob that. It might be of help to him. Beyond this, I promise I won't interfere."

But before the boys went into the guesthouse, Aunt Evelyn weakened a little. She asked them to help Bob as much as they could—and to keep him from doing anything too dangerous.

Inside the guesthouse, the boys found Bob concluding a conversation with Mrs. Wilson.

When he turned from the registration desk and saw them, he said, "Oh, no, guys, you've done enough for me already."

"What have you been up to?" Jack asked. "Did you find out where Maule lives?"

"I mean it," Bob said as they moved toward the door. "You've done enough. You shouldn't get mixed in this whole thing any more than you have."

"If we've done so much, you owe us something," Chip said. "Right?"

"Oh, of course. I'm aware of that."

"Then let us go along with you for the ride."

Jack nodded. "Yeah, Bob. That would be a great way of showing your appreciation." The boys hurried outside.

There Aunt Evelyn had a taxi waiting for them. Bending down, she stroked and patted Blaze, who looked up at her gratefully.

"Now, I want you to take Blaze with you," she told Bob. "Dogs are invaluable in trailing people."

"Good thing you didn't have more time than you did," Bob said to his aunt. "You'd have had the Marines here to back me up."

At the Somerset Hotel, which overlooked Hamilton Harbor, the desk clerk was thoughtful for a moment when Bob inquired about Stanley Maule. He then consulted a revolving card index.

"I thought so," he said. "Stanley Maule. Yes. He's checked out."

Bob and the boys stood for a moment in the lobby,

deciding on a course of action. Blaze took the opportunity to stretch out on a rug.

"There's a chance," Bob said, "he hasn't caught a plane yet."

"Yeah," Chip said eagerly, "and we might snag him before he does."

Jack then pointed out that Maule would hardly be flying back to New York, since he had apparently come to Bermuda on his own boat.

That started them searching for the *Lady Fair*.

Each time they saw a name on a boat, they would call it aloud.

"He probably took off," Bob said after a time. "Why should he stick around? He accomplished what he set out to do."

"Maybe he couldn't get his boat started," Chip suggested, trying to check Bob's sinking spirits. "He may still be around somewhere."

"A lot of things could keep him from leaving right away," Jack said. "Most important of all, if Maule ran off now he would be suspected of trying to cheat Bob out of his inheritance. And that would certainly wreck his chances of ever marrying Aunt Evelyn."

"That was the tip-off," Bob said, as though neither Jack nor Chip had spoken, "when we found out he'd checked out of his hotel. His next step would be to—"

Blaze's barking broke in on Bob.

"What's the matter, boy?" Chip asked Blaze.

"Hey, guys!" Jack exclaimed. "Look!"

A cabin cruiser rocked gently below them. Across her stern, in gold on a varnish brown, were the words *Lady Fair*.

They were astounded that Blaze could have known.

"Remember what my aunt said when she told us to take Blaze with us," Bob reminded them. "Maule could have kicked Blaze once or something. So he hasn't forgotten Maule's scent."

"Shhh!" Chip warned Blaze. "You did a good job. But now don't give us away."

"What are we going to do?" Jack asked curiously.

"You mean what am *I* going to do," Bob corrected.

An argument started as to whether or not Jack and Chip should go aboard the boat.

"All right," Bob gave in finally, "but remember, I'm

the one who's having the showdown with my good friend Maule."

They boarded the boat. It was so quiet that it seemed deserted. They tiptoed and spoke in whispers.

Before going down the companionway, they hesitated.

"It feels like we're going into a trap," Chip whispered.

"We'd better be careful," Jack said.

Exactly at that moment, Blaze squeezed between their legs and barked twice. They were loud, challenging barks.

22 *Showdown*

Jack, Chip, and Bob rushed headlong after Blaze. They were intent on one thing—silencing the dog. By the time they reached the bottom of the companionway, however, Blaze was barking at a man who was standing in the doorway of a cabin. The man was Maule.

"All right, simmer down," Chip said as he took Blaze by the collar.

Blaze whined. He knew he was being scolded, and he was asking to be forgiven.

"Gentlemen," Maule said expansively, "this is a pleasant surprise. My cabin is in a bit of a mess. But come in, come in."

Bob shook his head. "That won't be necessary."

"Is something wrong?" Maule asked. "I looked into the theft of the chart, Bob, but I—"

"That's not the theft I came to see you about."

Maule smiled, puzzled. "I don't—"

"You don't understand?" Bob snapped. "Don't give me that, Maule. You were on that dinghy and helped steal the footlocker. Now you're going to take me to the place where you got rid of it, or I'll—"

"Bob, Bob," Maule pleaded in a pained, perplexed way, "I don't know what you're talking about!"

"What have you got there?" Chip asked Blaze curiously.

Blaze had entered the cabin without anyone's noticing, for he was now dragging something from it, something that looked like a tablecloth.

When Maule saw the dog he turned pale. He frantically closed the door to his cabin. But he made a rapid recovery. "Let him play with the thing," he said good-naturedly. "It's of no value."

"Bob, I know I promised to keep out of this," Jack ventured, "but I think you ought to accept Mr. Maule's invitation. I mean, to go into his cabin and talk things over."

Maule smiled nervously. "Good idea," he said, still expansive. He spread his arms wide to herd them down the passageway. "But let's all go up on the deck, where there's plenty of room."

"Why don't you want us in your cabin?" Jack asked.

"Yeah. Why don't you?" Chip said belligerently.

"Why?" Maule answered, stalling. His anger suddenly flared. "Why? It's a small cabin. That's why." He smiled. "I'm sorry. I—I have been cooped up. I'm a little on edge. I'd like to go up on deck—and—and get some fresh air."

"I don't think we have to go anyplace," Bob said. "You haven't answered me yet, Maule. Are you going to take me—"

"Pardon me, Bob," Jack interrupted. "I've a hunch that what we're after"—he pointed at the cabin door—"is in there. You had the locker covered, Maule. And when you saw that Blaze had pulled the cover off, you got worried. That's when you closed the door, not wanting us to go in."

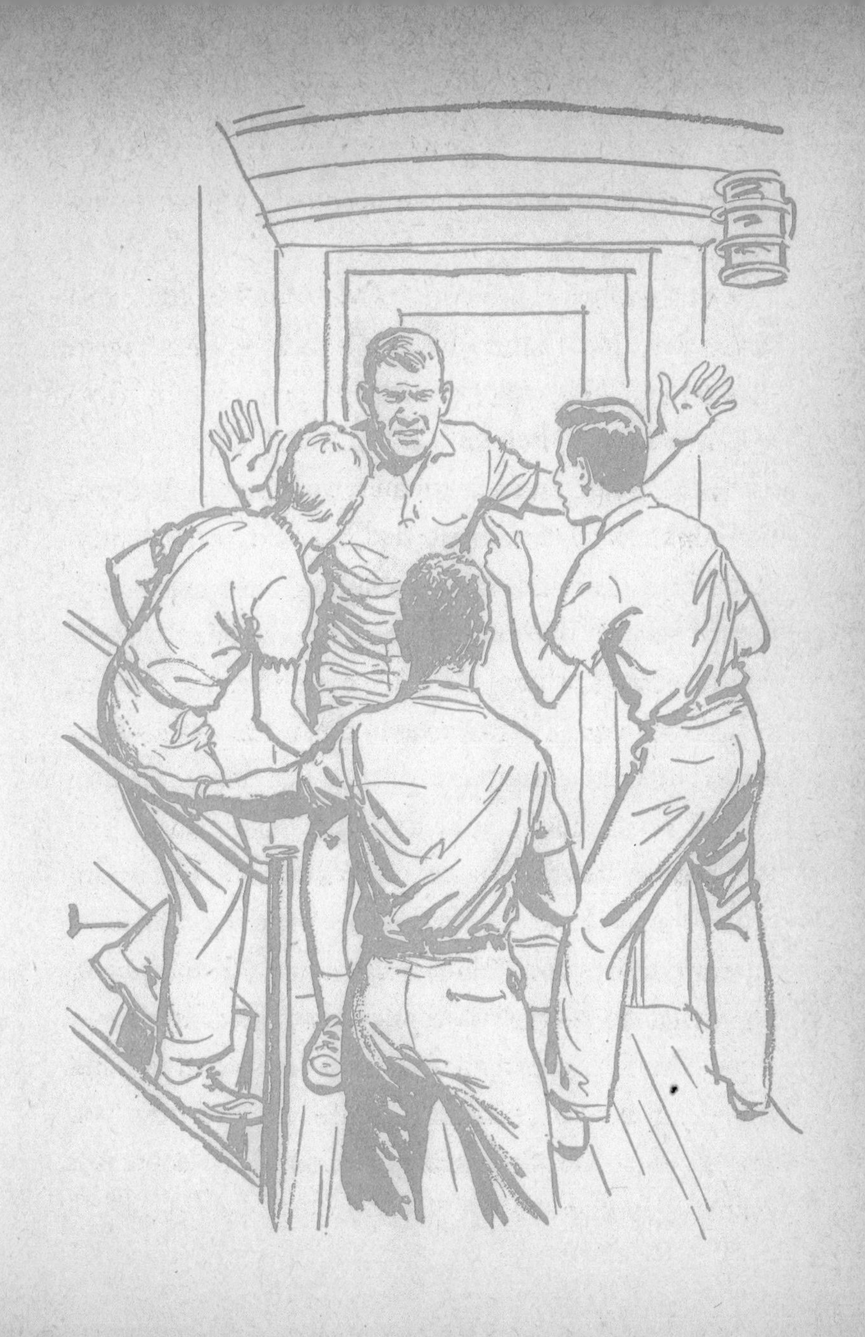

"So let's take a look," Bob said, making a move toward the cabin.

Maule stepped between Bob and the door. The color had again drained from his face. "This is my cabin!" he shouted. "You've no business—"

"Move away!" Bob said. In contrast to Maule's panicked shouting, Bob's command was quiet, but there was a knife edge to it. He jostled Maule to one side and opened the door. He walked straight to the footlocker, flipped open the loosened latch, raised the lid, and took out the gold figurine.

Just then two policemen came down the companionway, followed by Aunt Evelyn who had brought them.

"Are we in time?" Aunt Evelyn asked quickly.

"Yes, my dear," Maule said bitterly. "You're in time." He made no attempt to deny the charges against him as the boys and Aunt Evelyn explained to the police what had happened. While they talked, Reynolds—the reporter—appeared at the top of the companionway. He waited till the arrest was made, then marched off with the police and their prisoner.

"Don't look at me that way," Aunt Evelyn told Bob.

"At least I didn't bring the Marines—and you were worried I might."

"I didn't mind your bringing the cops," Bob said. "I'm glad you did." He looked down at the gold figurine in his hands, a giant with a Bermuda onion for a body. "Well," he said, "here it is. And if I didn't actually bring it up from the *Texas Queen,* I guess I did what Dad wanted me to do—proved what he wanted proved."

Aunt Evelyn moved to Bob and kissed his cheek. "I can't tell you how delighted I am," she said, "over what you've accomplished."

"Congratulations," Jack said.

"Yeah," Chip said. "Congratulations."

"You know, if it hadn't been for you guys," Bob told Jack and Chip, "I never would have made it. Here." He extended the figurine to them. "Take it. I've got to show my appreciation in some way."

Jack said, "Oh, no!" and Chip shook his head.

Bob laughed. "You'd better think it over. This thing's gold. It's worth a lot."

"It's too personal a thing, Bob," Jack said. "It means

too much to you to be giving it to us."

"That's why I want to give it to you," Bob insisted.

"You simply must reward them in some way," Aunt Evelyn said. "Lenny told me that they taught you how to dive—"

"That's another thing," Bob told the boys. "I haven't paid you yet for all those diving lessons. Did you keep track of the time? It's twelve bucks an hour. I haven't forgotten what we agreed on."

"It wasn't twelve," Jack corrected. "It was eight. Wasn't it, Chip?"

Chip nodded. "Don't go cheating yourself, Bob," he said.

When they reached the deck of the boat, they made a fuss over Blaze because of what he'd done.

In the middle of it, Bob said, "Say, why in the world do you think Maule held onto that locker? We all took it for granted that he would get rid of it."

"I know the answer," Aunt Evelyn said. *"Greed!* Stanley Maule had to open that locker first and make sure it didn't hold untold riches. It was the same greed, Bob, that compelled him to do all in his power to disinherit you. When he married me, according to plan, he wanted me to be as rich as possible."

Bob nodded absently. His thoughts had sped ahead to something else. "I just thought of something, fellows," he said eagerly. "How about helping me raise the *Texas Queen?* Do that, and she's all yours. How about it?"

"We'd sure like to help you bring her up," Jack said.

"A boat like that," Chip said in awe. "Golly. That's too much of a present."

"What's wrong with you guys?" Bob said. "The figurine was too personal. And now you're saying the *Texas Queen* is too big a present. They're hard to please, aren't they, Aunt Evelyn?"

"You work all that out," she said. "But I know that I'm going to give a little party tonight to celebrate."

The Bougainvillaea Room, in a wing of the guesthouse, was where Aunt Evelyn's party was held. Everyone who was in the least way connected with Bob's achievement was present. This included both Thomases; Mrs. Wilson; Samson, shaven for the occasion;

Reynolds, in Bermuda shorts, knee-length socks, and dinner jacket.

Bob led them in a toast to his father. "By making me get that figurine, Dad knew that he was giving me things that you just can't put down in a will. A sense of pride and perseverance—"

"And courage!" Aunt Evelyn called out. "I know, Bob, you're too modest to say it!"

"Here, here!" Reynolds shouted.

Lenny applauded loudly.

"And before I sit down," Bob said, "I want to give my special thanks to Jack and Chip Power for—"

Jack and Chip jumped up, interrupting Bob. Simultaneously the boys had seen their father standing in the doorway.

Mr. Power strode forward to meet his sons. He shook their hands.

"A party in my honor?" he asked, smiling. "How did you know I was coming?"

Chip went along with the gag. "Oh, we knew," he laughed.

"Seriously," Mr. Power said, "what's this all about?

I just heard you had special thanks coming to you."

"Oh, it's a long story, Dad," Jack said.

"Strange that this is always the case when I come back from a trip."

"Come on, Dad," Chip said, "I want you to meet everyone."

After the introductions, Bob asked Mr. Power if the boys could remain in Bermuda long enough to help him bring up the *Texas Queen*.

"Sounds dangerous," Mr. Power said, shaking his head.

As part of the evening's entertainment, Chip showed the underwater movie that he had shot. During the film he told all that had happened while Mr. Power was away.

"That's a fine film," Mr. Power told Jack and Chip warmly. "And I'm proud of what you did for your friend Bob Jillman."

"You've every reason to be proud," Aunt Evelyn said.

"You're right, Mother," Lenny said, grinning. "You're absolutely right."

Samson grunted. Then he went so far as to speak. "That pair got what it takes," he said. "Bob, too."

"Blaze!" Chip exclaimed. As he rushed out of the room he explained, "We forgot to bring him to the party!"

When Chip came back with the Dalmatian, Jack said excitedly, "You'll never guess, Chip, what Dad has decided to do."

"No kidding," Chip said. "Is he going to let us?"

"I'm not doing it for *them,*" Mr. Power was telling Bob, keeping a straight face and speaking loudly enough for his sons to hear. "I want to get pictures of that yacht being brought to the surface. It will make a terrific photographic essay!"

Happily Jack and Chip started punching each other in mock battle. They were going to bring up the *Texas Queen*. They were going to raise it from the burning ocean.

Blaze was pleased, too. He pranced around the boys and barked.

THE POWER BOYS

The Mystery of
THE HAUNTED SKYSCRAPER

The Mystery of
THE FLYING SKELETON

The Mystery of
THE BURNING OCEAN

The Mystery of
THE MILLION-DOLLAR PENNY

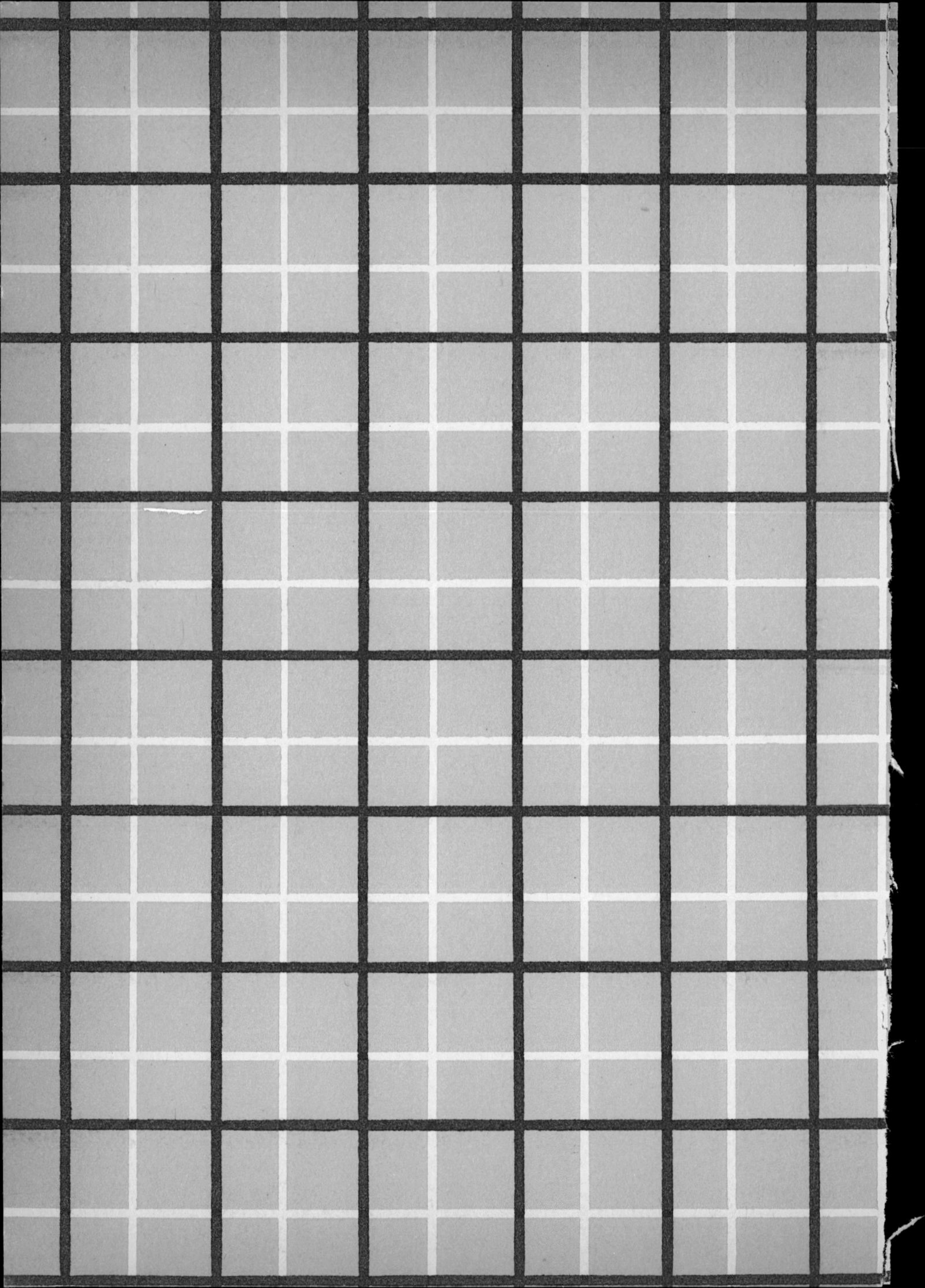